HEALING THE HERO

HEROES OF FREEDOM RIDGE

ELLE E. KAY

Healing the Hero

The Heroes of Freedom Ridge Book Three

Copyright © 2020 Elle E. Kay

All rights reserved.

No portion of this book may be reproduced in any form without permission
from the publisher, except as permitted by U.S. copyright law.

Cover Designer:
Amanda Walker, PA & Design Services
Editor:
Geesey Editorial Services

Faith Writes Publishing
266 Saint Gabriels Rd
Benton, PA 17814

Ebook ISBN: 978-1-950240-17-3
Paperback ISBN: 978-1-950240-18-0

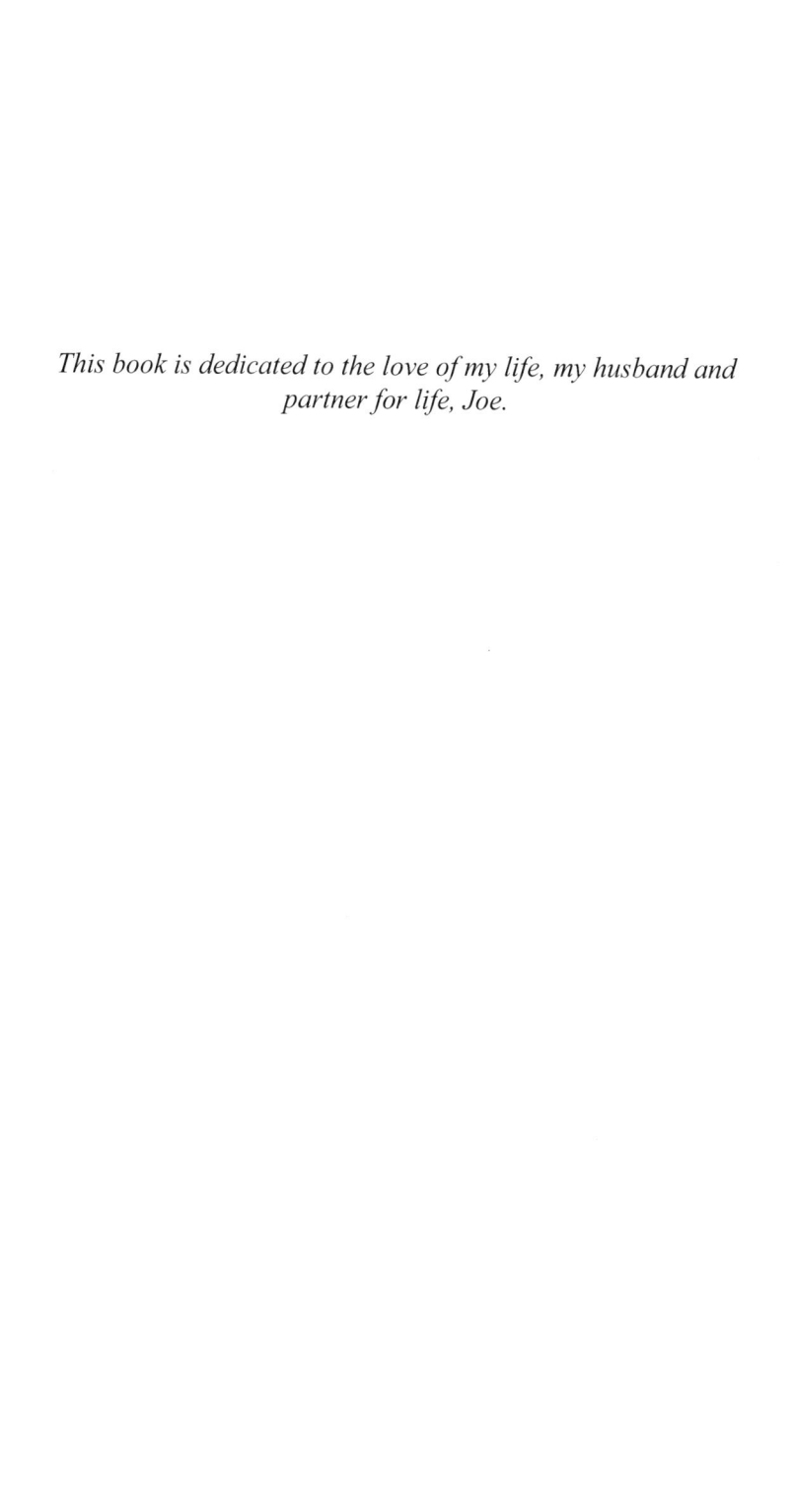

This book is dedicated to the love of my life, my husband and partner for life, Joe.

"O LORD my God, I cried unto thee, and thou hast healed me."

—*Psalms 30:2 (KJV)*

1

Standing in line at Mountain Mug with his rucksack on his shoulder, Dan felt the stares of the people around him. One older gentleman stuck out his hand. "Thank you for your service, young man."

Dan shook the man's hand. "Thank you for your support, sir."

"Danny, here's your coffee." Casey leaned across the counter with his order before he even placed it. It paid to be friendly with the barista. He picked up his coffee and inhaled the powerful aroma of the dark roast, tossed some cash on the counter, and gave Casey a brief wave. He was sure it was too hot to drink, but brought it to his lips anyway, took a sip, and burned his tongue. His watch read 2:50 p.m. He wouldn't have time to change into civilian clothes before interviewing his prospective chef. He walked around the reception desk and into the hotel management office space. If he didn't get to HR soon, he'd get an earful from Jeff Wallace.

A blond woman came out of the women's room and did a little turn like she was lost and trying to find her way. He laughed and kept walking. She abruptly turned around and slammed into his chest. His coffee flew out of his hand and drenched them both with scalding liquid. He pulled the fabric away from his skin to keep it from burning him. "Are you okay, ma'am? Are you burned?"

"I'm fine." Her gaze remained fixed on the floor. "I'm so sorry. I didn't mean... um..."

"May I help you find something, ma'am?"

He noticed her ears turning red. "Human Resources. I'm here for an interview."

"You're in luck. That's where I'm headed. Follow me." He glanced down at her coffee-stained blouse. "Unless you want to change first?"

"I wish I could, but I didn't bring any clothes other than a t-shirt and jeans for the plane ride home." He thought a clean t-shirt would be preferable to the stained blouse but kept his opinion to himself. Thankfully, the coffee stains were barely visible on his camouflage uniform. She fell into step beside him, and he showed her to the HR offices.

Spotting Mr. Wallace, Dan gave the woman one last cursory glance and a smile before making his way across the room to greet the HR Rep. "Good afternoon, Mr. Wallace."

"I didn't expect you to show up in your Army fatigues, Staff Sergeant." Jeff Wallace made eye contact.

"There was no time to change. It was the usual Army 'hurry up and wait' routine. We sat around Fort Bliss for hours waiting for our flight home."

He held out his hand, and Dan firmly shook it. "You haven't been home?"

"No time, sir."

"Thanks for coming in. It would've been a nightmare to

reschedule this interview. This chef flew in from Pennsylvania and plans to leave on a flight back tonight." The words struck him. Hadn't the woman who plowed into him mentioned something about a flight home? *Please, no. Don't let it be her.*

"Have a seat in the conference room. I'll see if she's here."

"Will do."

Less than a minute later, Mr. Wallace entered the room with the cute blond woman in the stained blouse at his side.

She groaned. "It's you."

"Yes, me. Sorry about earlier."

Her face turned crimson. "No." She attempted to straighten the wrinkles in her skirt. "It was my fault. I shouldn't have been so careless."

"I see you two have met."

"Not officially." Dan stood. "I'm Daniel Winchester, the restaurant manager for the Liberty Grille." He held out his hand, and she shook it.

Her eyes widened, and he admired their unique shade of blue. "I hadn't expected someone in uniform." She gestured at his fatigues.

"My apologies. I'm returning from AT, so I didn't have time to change out of my ACUs."

She raised one delicate eyebrow.

"Annual training. Army Reserves."

"And what are ACUs?"

"Oh, sorry. Army Combat Uniform."

"Ah." She tilted her head to the side. "I don't think I've heard my father use that abbreviation."

Mr. Wallace gestured for them to take their seats. "Shall we get started?"

"I didn't catch your name." Dan met the gaze of their interviewee.

She smiled. "Ashley. Ashley Castle."

"Ms. Castle, it's a pleasure to meet you."

THEY'D INTERVIEWED eight more so-called chefs before Friday afternoon rolled around, and by then, Dan was ready to call it quits, but they hadn't found the right person. Now he sat in a cramped office in HR overwhelmed by the odor of onions emanating from the nearby break room.

"Mr. Wallace, I'm not sure about Ashley Castle." He rose.

"Would you please call me Jeff?"

"Sorry, Jeff." Dan rocked back on his feet and sighed. "I'm not comfortable with this pick."

"She's the only qualified candidate we've interviewed, and we need a head chef. You have to choose someone." Jeff tapped his fingers on the desk. "We can't expect Carly to run the kitchen indefinitely. She's kept up to the best of her ability while we waited for you to return from AT."

"I can't believe Jacques walked out with no notice." Although, if he were being honest, he wasn't at all surprised. Jacques' given name was George, and he'd been an Army cook before going AWOL, getting dishonorably discharged, reinventing himself, and spending time in France. When Dan started at the resort, he and his chef had an unspoken agreement. Dan wouldn't mention the name change and stint in the Army if Jacques didn't mention that Dan was responsible for the deaths of the soldiers in his unit.

Jeff grimaced. "Well, I can believe it. The man was more temperamental than a caffeinated wolverine."

"Why can't we promote Carly and hire a new sous chef to work under her?"

"She's not qualified for the position, Dan. Give Ms. Castle a chance. She's got the education, the training, and the experience. She worked at one of the most prestigious restaurants in Philadelphia." Jeff made direct eye contact. "She's the right choice."

Dan frowned. "She wasn't a head chef at her previous job."

"The head chefs at most upscale big city restaurants sit behind desks and order around staff. They don't do much of the cooking. Those places run their restaurants differently than we do here. Trust me on this pick. I know what I'm doing."

Dan tipped his head back and looked at the ceiling. "Fine. Hire her."

"August 30th okay for a start date?"

"As good as any other." He let out a long exhale.

ASHLEY INHALED the aroma of fresh rosemary as she stirred the soupe du jour and watched Dan stroll through the kitchen.

Her first couple of weeks at the lodge, she'd been nervous

whenever he'd asked her to fix something for a customer. She'd worried that if she or one of her chefs cooked a customer's steak more or less than desired by the patron that he'd fire her on the spot. He hadn't. Dan had been easy-going. His goal was to keep the customer happy while trusting his staff to do their jobs with as little interference as possible.

Now instead of getting knots in her stomach every time Dan entered the kitchen, she admired the man. She noticed the way his dress shirt hugged his shoulders and the way his hair curled around his ears.

By the time her shift was over, she was glad for some space from her attractive boss. As much as she adored being around him, she was afraid she was forming an attachment to a man who had zero interest in her. Artificial light lit the parking lot, but as soon as she was off the lodge property, the thick darkness nearly swallowed the high beams on her Subaru.

She stopped at her mailbox and forced her thoughts away from her attractive boss. She had too much to do to pine away for a man who was unattainable. When she stepped inside the house, her cat, Ginger, greeted her by rubbing against her legs. She scooped the tabby up, kissed the top of her head, and asked "Did you behave while I was at work?" Receiving no answer from her feline friend, she fed her and filled her water.

Tossing the mail on the table, she sat down to sort through it. There were bills to pay and unless she wanted to keep using the old-fashioned checkbook and stamps approach, she'd need to set up her computer. She'd tried to use the bank's mobile app but hadn't found it intuitive.

A groan escaped. Computers were not her thing, but it'd been over two months since she'd moved to Colorado, so it was past time to face setting up her computer. She couldn't ask her younger brother to travel 1600 miles to set it up for

HEALING THE HERO

her.

After church next Sunday, she'd plan to call and ask him to walk her through the steps. In the meantime, she should at least unpack the components. She found her desktop computer in a box with some books. It was past its prime, so once she got another couple of paychecks, she'd consider purchasing a laptop, but for now she'd make-do with what she had.

An hour later, she finally located the cords, the mouse, and the keyboard. The screen was nowhere in sight. It had to be around somewhere. She'd look again in the morning.

Her thoughts drifted to Dan once again, and she pondered what he might be doing. He was probably reading a book. He seemed like the intellectual type. It was another reason she didn't stand a chance with him. Her books consisted of her Bible, some commentaries, and cookbooks. An avid reader, she was not.

DAN STARED out over the empty dining room and pictured the place packed with tourists for the upcoming ski season. The room was cavernous, too massive for the smaller crowds they had off-season, so they kept it closed off part of the year. He hoped Ashley would be up to coordinating the cooking for so many. When he'd hired her in August, he hadn't been confident she'd be able to do the job, but she'd proven herself, and she had an amiable relationship with her sous chef, which put her far above her predecessor in his book. Jacques may have been a brilliant chef, but his attitude made it impossible for any of the kitchen staff to get along with him.

Jeff Wallace strolled into the dining room. "Morning,

Dan."

"Good to see you this morning, Mr. Wallace." Dan shook the other man's hand.

"How many times do I have to tell you to call me Jeff?" He raised his brows.

"Sorry, Jeff. It's a hard habit to break."

"I noticed you through the glass when I was walking by outside. Thought we might chat a minute." He straightened up and made direct eye contact. "I think I found you a junior chef."

"That's fabulous news." Dan smiled. "When can he or she start?"

"I told Thomas I'd try to arrange an interview with you for this afternoon. I realize Chef Castle will need time off soon."

"Working six days a week is too much for anyone."

"I agree."

"Carly is great, but she can't be expected to run the kitchen without help."

"True."

"Once the seasonal help starts everything should go smoothly with Ashley in charge and Carly filling-in in her absence, but until then, we need that junior chef to ease the workload when one or the other of them takes time off."

"You mentioned that Ashley wants Sundays off, correct?"

"And Wednesday nights." A muscle jumped in Dan's jaw. "She's religious."

"The young man is somewhat inexperienced since he's recently graduated from culinary school, but he's eager to learn and willing to take direction. Plus, he's a local, so there's less chance of him leaving the moment we get him trained."

"Sounds like an adequate choice. I don't need to meet him."

"You don't?"

"No. Tell him it'll be a trial period. Sixty days will work. If he doesn't work out, we let him go, but it'll keep me from making a snap judgment before I've seen how he handles the pressures of the kitchen. If that works for you, I mean?"

"Sure. We can do that. Do you think Ms. Castle will mind training him?"

"Yes, I do." He chuckled. "She'll come around though, and Carly will do most of his training."

"What should I give him as a start date?"

"How's two weeks from today? November 15th at ten o'clock?"

"That works. I'll make the offer."

2

Ashley jumped back a step when she looked up to find Dan staring at her. "What?" She swiped her sleeve across her cheek. "Do I have flour on my face or something?"

"No. You look fine." His eyes crinkled at the corners. Turning down the volume on her bluetooth speaker, he kept his eyes focused on her.

"Did you need something, boss?"

"I'd like to meet with you and Carly to discuss the menu for the upcoming season."

"Sure." She moved to the sink and washed the dough off her hands. "What time?"

A lock of sandy blond hair fell across his forehead, and he pushed it back into place. "How's eleven?"

"Won't work."

"My bad. I wasn't thinking of the lunch rush." He tapped

his finger against his bottom lip. "What time works for you and Carly?"

"She doesn't start until ten and that's cutting it close to our busy time. After we close might be best." She dried her hands and leaned back against the counter in an attempt to look relaxed.

"Quarter past nine okay?" he asked.

"That'll work." She briefly made eye-contact before lowering her gaze. He sauntered across the kitchen, and she allowed herself to stare until he disappeared through the doorway.

Dan's smile occupied her thoughts until Carly arrived.

"You'll never guess what happened on my way in." Carly shouted across the cavernous kitchen as she breezed in. "It's quiet in here. What happened to your music?"

"The boss turned it down."

"Oh."

Carly reached for the knob and turned it back up. "I wish you'd listen to something more mainstream."

"I don't like that stuff."

"Anyway, don't you want to guess what happened?"

Ashley shook her head. "I'd rather not."

"Fine. I'll tell you." There was a gleam in her eye. "I got in a fender-bender."

"I'm certain I haven't seen anyone get so excited about a car accident before." Ashley lifted an eyebrow.

Carly shrugged on her chef's jacket and twisted her purple

hair into a bun securing it with a scrunchie.

Ashley shivered. "We have a locker room for that. Hair and kitchens don't mix."

Rolling her eyes, Carly said, "The locker room is a glorified supply closet, and my hair is back now, so there's no point. So, the man who rear-ended my car was drop-dead gorgeous, and he asked me out."

"Only you can turn a car crash into a dating opportunity."

"You should date. You work too much."

"I don't have time to date. Dan needs to hire a junior chef before I can take time off."

As if she'd conjured him by mentioning his name, Dan sauntered through the kitchen flashing them one of his signature smiles as he headed into the dining room. Ashley's eyes followed him until he disappeared from sight.

"You could date Danny-boy," Carly said.

"Our boss?" Ashley felt the heat rise to her cheeks. "I don't think so."

"Why not?"

"We work together for one. Besides, I'm not his type. He goes for women like Ivy. She could be in one of those swimsuit magazines. I'd never measure up to her."

"There's a reason he isn't with her anymore."

"Exactly. And if he dumped her, I don't stand a chance."

Carly grinned. "Don't sell yourself short."

"Dan and I are just friends."

"You shouldn't let him friend-zone you when you've been crushing on him since you arrived in town."

"Have not."

"Have too."

"Maybe a little, but he's way out of my league."

"Danny has a thing for blonds." She winked. "I'll bet he loves your golden locks."

"Where did you hear he had a thing for blonds?'"

"I overheard Max razzing him about it." She disappeared into the walk-in refrigerator and returned a minute later, her arms laden with jars. "Besides, Ivy's a blond."

Ashley wanted to laugh. Ivy's platinum-blond hair was no more natural than her acrylic nails or her fake eyelashes. She chastised herself for being catty and turned back to her sous chef. "We should stop wasting time and get to work."

Carly saluted her. "You've got it, boss."

"Dan wants us to meet him to discuss the proposed menu for ski season."

"Did he give you a time?"

"We're meeting him at nine-fifteen."

"Did you figure out how you want to overhaul the menu?"

"I think so, but I'd appreciate it if you'd take a look at my ideas sometime this afternoon to make sure they sound appealing before I show them to the boss."

"You've got it."

Ashley removed the folded paper from her apron. "Here you go."

Carly unfolded the sheet of paper and scanned it quickly before stuffing it in her back pocket. "Looks terrific at first glance. I'll give you more input after I have time to think it over."

DAN CLOSED his office door with more force then necessary. They'd turned up that blasted gospel music again. There was a time when he would've enjoyed it, but these days it got under his skin.

"Everything okay in there, Danny?" his assistant asked over the intercom.

He pressed the button to answer. "Everything is fine. Sorry, Sabrina. I didn't mean to shut the door so hard."

His mind drifted to Ashley. The woman was far too quiet. She was a tiny thing. At least a foot shorter than his 6'3" frame. There was an adorable sprinkling of freckles across the bridge of her nose. She was cute, but not a traditional beauty like Ivy. He derided himself for thinking about an employee in a romantic light. They could be friends, but nothing more.

He ran a hand over his hair. He needed to see a barber, but with the season ready to descend upon them, there was no time for haircuts. Preparations needed to be made before the skiers and snowboarders arrived in full force.

A single knock on his door announced a visitor before his ex-fiancée slid inside and perched on the edge of his desk inches from where he sat. Her cloying perfume assaulted his senses, so he slid his chair back to put some distance between them.

"What do you need, Ivy?"

"Can't I simply want to see you?"

"No." He scowled. "Don't you have tables to wait?"

"My shift doesn't start for another fifteen minutes. I was hoping to catch a moment alone with you before I started." She twisted a strand of white-blond hair around her finger and pouted.

"I don't have time for this."

"When will you have time? We could go out after work."

"I don't think so."

Her bottom lip quivered. "Are you ever going to forgive me?"

"I've moved on. You should do the same."

"How can I move on when I'm in love with you?"

"So in love with me that you hooked up with Gage while I was deployed? Let me move on with my life. I gave you this job, but you knew the conditions. Keep things professional or go find another job."

"I'll claim sexual harassment if you fire me."

"That's ridiculous. If anyone's being harassed, it's me."

A slow smile formed on her face. "That's not what I'll tell everyone." She hopped off his desk and took a step closer. She ran her fingernail down his neck and across his collarbone. "Which one of us do you think the local news will believe?"

"How could I have been so wrong about you?" he asked.

She shrugged. "Shall I expect your company after work?"

"I'm working late."

"Suit yourself. I'm sure I can find someone willing to spend the evening with me."

"I'll bet you will."

~

ASHLEY SETTLED at the table in the break room with Carly by her side. "Did you get a chance to review the proposed changes to the menu?"

Carly leaned back in her seat. "I did."

"What did you think?"

"I love it. Well, except..."

"Except what? What's wrong with it?" Ashley blinked several times.

"Nothing is wrong with it. I'm simply not sure pan-seared Muscovy duck breast will be a big seller. You might be better off choosing something like Slow-Roasted Bison."

"You may be right." She scratched out the duck. "What do you think of substituting Rocky Mountain Elk T-Bone?"

"That sounds like a winner." Carly gave her the thumbs up sign. "I'm glad we're finished for the night."

"We're not finished. We still have a meeting with the boss."

"I meant finished cooking. Spending time with Danny-boy is more pleasure than work."

"Stop." Ashley felt her cheeks warm. "I don't know why you insist on calling him that."

"What? It's cute."

"I'm not sure he'd agree."

Dan appeared in the doorway. "Which he?"

Ashley felt heat rise to her face. "Um."

"Ashley's worried you'll find out I call you Danny-boy."

"You've been calling me that since you were eight. I'm used to it."

Ashley narrowed her eyes in Carly's direction. Carly was too young to have gone to school with Dan, so she wondered how they knew each other. Freedom was a small town, maybe everyone knew one another.

"You two ready to meet? It's five minutes early, but if you're ready, we might as well get started."

"Sure." Ashley stood and followed Carly and Dan from the room.

Carly put her hand on his bicep, and Ashley had to fight the envy that surged through her veins. "So, Danny, I heard Ivy talking about the two of you getting back together. Say it ain't so?"

"It ain't so."

"That's a relief. I've been thinking about the ideal girl to set you up with."

"No set-ups. I'm staying single."

"That would be a waste." Carly looked him up and down.

He laughed. "We have work to do." He sank into a chair at a round table in the corner of his office. "I hope you won't mind if this meeting goes late. I'll order us a pizza or something. I'm trying to avoid someone."

Carly giggled. "I have a date, but I'm not necessary to this meeting, so I'll leave the two of you to finish the planning when it's time for me to split."

"Is that okay with you, Ash?" Dan asked

"Sure." Ashley looked down at the wrinkled paper in her shaking hands. "If you can stay for a few minutes, that'll be okay."

"If you have to go, too. I'll understand." Dan frowned. "We can do this tomorrow before work."

"No. It's fine. I can stay as long as you need me to."

⁓

THEY'D BARELY begun discussing the menu changes when Carly scooted out.

"I'd hoped Carly would stay longer." Ashley met Dan's gaze.

He smiled. "Why is that?"

"No reason."

"You have the details of your proposal together if in a somewhat unorthodox fashion." He glanced at her wrinkled paper and winked. "I'm not sure I've ever received a menu proposal on a folded piece of notebook paper before."

"I don't have my computer set up yet." She tried to smooth out the wrinkles in her paper.

"Why is that? Are we working you too hard?"

"No. The hours are fine."

He squinted at her. "The hours are brutal. I should know

we've been working the same schedule."

"I'll try to come up with something more professional next time."

"What makes you think there will be a next time?"

"I assumed you'd want to change the menu every year."

He cocked his head to the side. "Most likely, but I meant what makes you think you'll still be here."

"Why would I go?"

"Oh, I don't know. Maybe you'll decide you miss home and leave Colorado."

"That's not in my plans." She glanced toward the door, and he wondered if she was looking to escape the conversation.

"That's what I want to hear. The restaurant needs stability. Being forced to change chefs isn't convenient for us, and it can hurt the reputation of Liberty Grille." He leaned across the table and took the paper from her shaking hands. He placed his left hand over her right hand and made eye contact. "What are you nervous about, Ashley? I may be your boss, but we're friends. Aren't we?"

"Yeah. Of course, we are." She bit her bottom lip.

"Relax." He squeezed her hand. "I'll order us a pizza and we can hang out in the lounge. It'll be more comfortable to sit in there by the fire."

―

ASHLEY SAT beside the fire reveling in its warmth. Barely an inch separated her from Dan. Earlier when he'd placed his hand on top of hers, she'd struggled to breathe. Now the sensations swirling around inside her were stronger than ever.

He leaned back and draped his arm across the back of the leather sofa, and the faint spicy scent of his cologne reached her. She inhaled deeply.

"This is nice," he said.

She tucked her hair behind her ears. "It is."

"Do you mind if we eat before we get back to our planning session?"

"Not at all. I'm starving."

He opened the pizza box, and the aroma of garlic and oregano set her stomach to growling in anticipation. He took out two slices, and after placing them on paper plates, he handed her one. "You'll like Valentino's pizza. It's not what you'd get in your neck of the woods, but it's the best we have in the area."

"I'll admit I'm a slight pizza snob, but it's nothing compared to my disdain for the cheesesteaks around here. Only Philadelphia cheesesteaks will do." She took a bite. "This is not bad."

"Add them to the menu."

"What?"

"Cheesesteaks."

"No way. You don't have Amoroso rolls. I will not serve a Philadelphia Cheesesteak on anything else."

"Fly them in. It'll be perfect for the other cheesesteak snobs that visit Freedom Ridge."

"Sure. Why not? If you're willing to bear the extra expense of flying in rolls, I'm happy to add cheesesteaks to the lunch menu."

"Maybe you could add some other Philadelphia favorites."

"Let's not overdo it. I don't think scrapple will sell that well here."

He scrunched up his nose.

"Don't knock it until you try it. Habbersett scrapple is delicious."

"I'll take your word for it." He took a big bite of his pizza.

"Any luck finding a junior chef?"

"We hired someone Monday. I hope he works out." Dan rubbed his chin.

"Why wouldn't he?"

"Jeff recommended him after his HR interview. We'll have to see. I told him I didn't need to interview him myself. I think it's better if we test his abilities on the job. He'll have a sixty-day probation period."

"I'm glad you didn't do that with me. I don't think I'd have relocated from Pennsylvania for a probationary position."

"This guy is a local. He attended culinary school in Denver and got back in town in May."

"That's a considerable amount of time without no job."

"I'm not sure he was unemployed. I didn't ask." He stared into the fire for a moment before picking up her sample menu. He glanced over it again. "The only thing missing is a signature dish."

"A what?"

"We need something special. You can choose anything on the menu or add something new. Make it something you'd order yourself if you were visiting a restaurant. A favorite dish."

"How about surf and turf?"

"Too generic."

"What if we swap the lobster for salmon?"

"That'll do if we add a special sauce for the salmon?"

"How about a honey sriracha glaze?"

"Sounds delicious. We'll call it Chef Ashley Castle's Surf & Turf. In parenthesis we'll type: fillet mignon and honey sriracha glazed salmon served with the vegetable of the day and garlic mashed potatoes. Does that work?"

"If you're sure you want my name on the menu? I don't see the point."

"I'm sure." He grinned. "I guess that's settled."

3

"No way, Dan." She shook her head even though he couldn't see her. "I'm beginning to regret answering my phone."

"It'll be fun."

"You know perfectly well that I don't ski, and I don't snowboard. Forget it. Call one of your guy friends to go with you."

"We'll go snow-tubing instead. You'll love it. The next thing you know, you'll be begging for ski lessons."

"Let this go."

"Not a chance." She could hear the smile in his voice. "I'll pick you up in twenty minutes."

"Make it thirty. I just got home from church, so I need to change my clothes."

"See you shortly."

What was she thinking agreeing to snow-tube with Dan? Her feelings for him were confusing enough without spending extra time with him. Being Dan's friend was pure torture. The worst part was knowing he could never see her as someone with romantic potential. It would be in her best interest to ignore Carly's promptings and forget about anything more than friendship with him.

Sorting through her sweaters, she smiled. An entire day with Daniel Winchester. What sane girl would say no to that? She dressed in her softest pink sweater and a pair of comfy jeans. She hoped she was dressed all right and would be able to rent anything else she needed at the resort.

When the doorbell rang, she hurried to the door and opened it. "Hi. Come on in."

"Hey." He clasped his hands behind his back. "You look nice. I love the fluffy sweater. It's much different from your black slacks and white apron."

She laughed. "I need to grab my hiking boots."

"Don't you have snow boots?" His gaze traveled to the cardboard boxes she hadn't unpacked. He probably thought she was a slob. Ginger leapt on top of the pile of boxes and stared down their guest.

"Not yet." She gestured toward the cat. "That there is my cat, Ginger."

"She's a beauty." He looked in the tabby cat's direction before making eye contact with her again. "Maybe you should add snow boots to your shopping list."

She took a step back and held her hands up. "I haven't had time to buy any. You keep me too busy at work."

"True." He smiled. "But you need to make it a priority. You're going to need them up here on the mountain."

"I will." She hurried off and returned a minute later with hiking boots in hand. It took her a couple of minutes to lace them up, and then they were on their way.

"Thanks for doing this." He stuffed his hands in his pockets. "I need a day out on the slopes."

"Why not go with one of your buddies?"

"I didn't want to go with one of them. I want to go with you."

Was he trying to be charming, or did he mean his words? He'd called her, so maybe he did want to spend time with her. Now if only she could keep herself from acting like a fool.

⁂

ASHLEY'S EYES widened when Dan stopped the truck in town at Freedom Mountaineering. "What do we need here?"

"You need snow boots."

"Now?" She wrinkled her nose.

"Now is as good a time as any."

As he and Ashley entered the store, Aiden was coming out.

"Hey Aiden. Have you met our head chef, Ashley?"

"I've seen her around the lodge, but we haven't been introduced."

"Ashley, Aiden here is a snow-boarding instructor at the lodge."

"Nice to officially meet you, Aiden."

"You too." Aiden asked. "Heading out to the slopes?"

Dan put his arm around Ashley's shoulders. "I'm taking

Ashley tubing."

"Convince her to take some boarding lessons."

"I'm sure she'd be a natural, but we'll start with tubing."

Aiden took a step back into the store so the door could close.

"What are you up to today?" Dan asked.

"I have a lesson. Stopped in to pick up some wax for my board. We don't have the kind I like at the lodge."

"Have fun today." Ashley smiled.

Gage headed toward them, and Aiden shuffled back out the door. "What can I help you with today?" He focused his attention on Ashley.

"She needs snow boots," Dan supplied the answer for her.

Gage's eyes lit with challenge when he met Dan's gaze. "I'll be glad to help you with that, Miss." He winked at Ashley. "Follow me."

Ashley chose a pair of pink boots with a soft fur lining, and Gage retreated into the back to see if they had her size. Dan followed him into the back. "What do you think you're doing?"

"What are you talking about, Danny-boy?"

"Just because I let your sister call me that, doesn't mean you can get away with it."

"You're not supposed to be back here, bud."

"Stop coming on to Ashley."

"I don't know what you're talking about, Danny. I'm simply helping a customer."

"Get her the boots, so we can get out of here."

"Yes, sir." Gage saluted.

"And stop being a smart-alec."

"Go back out to your little girlfriend. I'll be out with her boots in a minute or two."

Dan hustled back to the main area where Ashley was sitting on a bench with her stocking feet tucked under her waiting for the promised boots."

"Sorry about that."

"What was that about?"

"Nothing."

"I sense a history, but I'll leave it alone."

"Wise idea." He clenched his jaw. "I hadn't realized Gage would be here. His dad owns the shop, but he only works when he feels like it."

"Oh."

"He's Carly's older brother."

"I wasn't aware she had a brother."

"I'm surprised she hasn't mentioned him. She idolized him when she was younger."

"These days, I think Carly focuses every ounce of her attention on cooking and guys. She doesn't leave much energy for talking about family or much else."

He shook his head slightly. "Carly's a good kid even if she is a bit on the wild side."

ELLE E. KAY

∽

ASHLEY COULD see her breath in the crisp mountain air as she walked beside Dan to the gondola that would take them to the top of the mountain. On the way up, she could see for miles in every direction. The beauty of the snow covered peaks was captivating, and having Dan beside her made the experience enchanting.

When they arrived, he grabbed a tube and handed it to her before getting one for himself. From there they took something he called a magic carpet. It was similar to the moving walkways they had at some airports.

Once up top, she tried to calm the nerves in her stomach. She'd never done any winter sports. The closest she'd been to doing this was taking her sled down a steep hill in her neighborhood when she was ten. Even then, she'd thought she was taking her life in her hands. She watched as children flew down the mountainside on tubes with broad smiles on their faces. If they could do it, so could she.

Dan showed her how to keep their tubes together. He held the strap from hers and she clung to his, wrapping the nylon strap around her hand she held onto both handles. A moment later, they were flying down the mountain, and she felt herself grinning like a kid on an amusement park ride.

When they came to a stop at the bottom, she tried to stand, but fell out of her tube.

Dan helped her up. "What did you think?"

"That was fun."

"Want to go a few more times?"

"Are you kidding?" She grinned. "Let's go."

After a few more runs down the mountain they made their way inside the lodge to warm up by the fire. She took a seat while Dan ordered them some warm drinks from Ty at Mountain Mug.

Casey sank down beside her on the sofa. "Funny seeing you here today with mister charming."

"He needed someone to hang-out with, and I was a convenient choice. Don't read more into it than that."

"You might want to tell him that. He's shooting daggers my way for sitting in his spot beside you." Casey stood.

"You off already, Case?" Dan asked as he handed Ashley a hot chocolate. She sipped her drink, savoring the rich liquid.

"It's after three, hotshot." Casey's eyes lit with humor. "I'm heading out. Got me a date with a tourist."

"Have a nice time." Ashley waved as Casey walked away.

~

MONDAYS WERE bad enough, but Mondays in November the week before tourist season took off in full force was brutal. Dan spent the day going over requests for banquet rooms and private dining events. The reservation requests had overwhelmed his hostess, Amanda. It got to the point where he had to ask his assistant, Sabrina, to field them, so the hostess could seat customers as they came in rather than spend her whole day on the telephone.

It was after midnight when he finally arrived home, and all he wanted to do was sink into bed and flip on the television.

He pulled his F150 into the driveway. The news hadn't

mentioned snow in the forecast, but the air felt like it. If he were a betting man, he'd bet on an inch or two of fresh powder by morning. Once inside he detected a faint hint of women's perfume along with the usual odor of stale air from his closed up house. Strange. Must be his imagination. He should crack a window and let fresh air into his abode.

He emptied his pockets onto the kitchen counter and crossed the room to the stairwell. Odd. He would've sworn he'd left the hall light on upstairs. Could've burned out. When he reached the top of the stairs, he noticed the switch was off. Maybe he hadn't left it on after all. After a quick shower, he approached his bed. It was made. He hadn't made it. Never did. His sister must be in town. She was the only other person with a key, so it was the only plausible explanation. He'd text her in the morning and find out what she'd been doing at his place.

The smell of fabric softener greeted him when he leaned back on his pillows. His sister washed his sheets? She must think he was a pig who couldn't fend for himself. He'd have to let her know that while he appreciated the gesture, it was unnecessary. He was more than capable of doing his own laundry. Scrolling through the channels, he found a classic sitcom and settled in for the night.

"BETH, DON'T mess with me." Dan leaned back in his office chair and stared at the ceiling.

"Why would I mess with you?"

"You're honestly not in town?"

"No, and even if I was, I can promise you that washing your sheets wouldn't be at the top of my list of priorities. I can barely keep up with our laundry." She sighed. "Maybe Mother hired a housekeeper for you."

"Mother doesn't have a key to my house."

"About that..."

"You didn't."

"She asked. What was I going to say?"

"Maybe you could've said something like, 'Ask Daniel yourself if you want a key to his house.'"

"No way." She snickered. "You want to tick Mother off, you go ahead, but I'm not getting in the middle."

"You got in the middle when you handed over your key to my place." He sighed. "But at least now, I can deduce what happened. You're obviously correct. She hired a housekeeper."

"Maybe you should ask Mother about it."

"Yeah. I will." He wasn't sure he wanted to ask his mom, if she said it wasn't someone she hired, he would have to consider the possibility that he was losing his mind. Burglars didn't break in and clean, so it had to be a housekeeper, didn't it? He'd remember if he'd done any of that stuff himself. "I'd better get back to work. Thanks for setting my mind at ease even if you did betray my trust." He held back a chuckle. He had to believe that his mother was behind the strange happenings.

"Stuff it, Danny."

"Goodbye."

"Wait. One more thing."

"What's that?"

"I'm coming to town in two weeks for Daddy's birthday."

"Oh?"

"Mom wants you to throw a big shindig at the lodge."

"With less than three weeks' notice? Wonderful. Why do you always know about this stuff before I do?"

"Because you avoid our mother."

"That may prove difficult now that she has a key to my house."

"Touché."

4

Carly leaned against the counter and twirled her silicone spatula. "I have another date with Sean tonight after work."

"You do?"

"Can you believe it?"

"Two dates with the same man may be a record for you."

Carly stuck her tongue out at Ashley. "Casey said you were in here with Danny-boy on Sunday. What were you two doing, and how did we get through a whole week without you mentioning it?"

"We went snow-tubing."

"Together?" Carly clapped her hands. "I want every detail."

"There's nothing to tell. We had fun, but it was a friend thing. Don't read more into it. Okay?"

"If you say, so." She bounced up and down on her toes. "But I've seen how he looks at you when he thinks nobody is watching, and he's never asked me to go snow-tubing."

"Please don't do that. My heart can't take it." Ashley massaged her neck with her left hand. "Sometimes I get mixed signals from him, but he has a flirtatious nature. He's made it clear we are friends. Nothing more."

"But —"

"Why didn't you ever mention your brother? I met him on Sunday."

"You did, huh?"

"I haven't seen him in here."

Carly let out an exaggerated sigh. "My brother has a reputation as a player. He's calmed down lately now that he's found God, but I didn't want him to come on to you, so I didn't introduce you to him."

"You were protecting me from your brother?"

"You're a much better fit with Danny."

"How sisterly of you. I'm sure your brother would be thrilled to find out you're warning single women away."

"Not all of them. Only the ones I love like sisters."

Dan entered the kitchen from the back hall, and they both stopped talking.

"Why do I sense I'm interrupting?"

"Maybe it's because you are." Carly tried to hip bump him but hit closer to his knees.

He laughed and turned to face Ashley. "Hey."

She set down the ladle she was using to drizzle cranberry glaze onto plates of ham. "Yeah?"

"Smells good in here." The side of his mouth turned up in

a half grin. "Everything good?"

Her hand fluttered over her heart, and she nodded. Everything wasn't good. She was confused as could be, but if she didn't verbalize the yes, it wasn't a lie, right?

"I've got a huge favor to ask." His smile widened showing off the dimple in his left cheek.

"What's that?" She raised an eyebrow.

"There is going to be an event in one of the banquet rooms on November 20th, and I need your help planning it."

"They called this late, and you accepted the booking?"

"It's for my father's sixtieth birthday."

"You're throwing the party?"

"Technically, my mother is, but she wants it here at the lodge, so that means you and I are."

She sunk into her stool and propped her head up with her fist. "Great."

"You don't have to sound so enthused."

"No. It's fine. It's just that I still don't have my computer set up, so I'll have to do everything by hand."

"You can use one of the computers here."

"I don't have time to work on it while I'm here."

"It's work related. You should get paid for your time."

"I'd rather do the research at home."

"What is there to research? Pick two main courses and ask Van to choose a few desserts." He glanced toward Van, the pastry chef.

Van nodded. "I'll take care of the desserts."

She frowned. "There's more to planning a menu than choosing two main courses."

"I'll help you narrow it down. Let's grab a bite to eat after work?"

She should say no. Why couldn't she bring herself to say no? Time alone with him was a bad idea. "Sure. Why not?"

"Great. We can scoot out of here early, and let Carly handle the cooking. I'll meet you at the Mountain Mug at seven."

"Are you sure?"

"You deserve a break. We'll grab a coffee for the road and make it to Evelyn's in time for dinner."

"You want to go out to dinner with me?"

"We both need to eat. Don't we?"

"I suppose so, but do you think we could go somewhere more casual?" she glanced down at her uniform.

Dan grinned. "Sure." He left the kitchen by way of the dining room, straightening his tie as he did.

Carly turned to face her with a giant grin on her face. "See! I told you he was interested."

"He is not interested. The dinner is to plan his father's birthday celebration. It's not a date."

"Maybe not, but it's a start." Carly's forehead crinkled. "Why didn't you agree to go to Evelyn's?

"It's expensive and I don't have clothes with me."

"I'm sure Danny boy would've paid."

"Give it up, Carly." Ashley lifted her ladle and got back to work. "It's not going to happen. He's in Ivy's league, not mine."

Carly took the ladle from her hand. "Give me that. Go get ready for your date. I'll finish up here."

"He's not meeting me for another hour. Besides you've got your own date tonight, so maybe you should worry about that."

"Go get ready." She tilted her head to the side. "Brush your hair. Pinch your cheeks. Do whatever you city girls do to gussy up for a big date."

"I'm not a city girl. I'm from the suburbs." Ashley crinkled her nose.

"Same difference."

"Fine. I'm going."

Carly lifted her chin and drizzled the remaining glaze over the ham. "I'm looking forward to the full staff returning. It'll be nice to have someone else to do the plating. That way I can focus on cooking."

"Presentation matters."

"Taste matters more." Carly pointed to the door. "Now, go!"

THE AROMA of fresh ground coffee greeted Dan as he approached the counter at Mountain Mug. Ashley was ordering her favorite latte, peppermint peaks mocha.

"The usual, Danny?"

"Please." The barista handed him his dark roast black coffee before fixing Ashley's drink. "Thanks, Casey."

"I see who her favorite is." Ashley glanced his way from under lowered lids before returning her stare to her feet.

"It's a perk of drinking black coffee. They squeeze you in before they fix the fancy fru fru drinks." He cleared his throat. "It's pretty warm for November, do you want to take a ride out to Hidden Lake? We can sit at a picnic table and drink our coffees while we talk about the party."

"Okay."

"Afterwords, we can grab a bite to eat at Valentino's unless you'd rather go somewhere else."

"Valentino's is fine."

He opened the truck door for her, and then climbed in on the driver's side. The ride to the lake passed in comfortable silence, and he was grateful for that. He'd felt her eyes on him as he'd walked through the kitchen earlier in the day. When he'd turned to smile in her direction, she'd quickly turned back to her work. He didn't want their working relationship to be awkward, but it seemed to be moving in that direction. Maybe befriending her had been a mistake. It was a difficult balancing act maintaining friendships with employees. If he had any sense, he'd stop spending time with her outside of the restaurant, but the truth was, he liked her and wanted her in his life as more than an employee.

He glanced over at Ashley who seemed mesmerized by the dusting of snow on the tall evergreens shadowing the road. "Pretty isn't it?"

"Reminds me of home."

"It does?"

"It's not so shocking. We have pine trees in Pennsylvania. Tall ones right in our yard."

"I thought you lived in an urban area."

"Suburban. My parents live about thirty minutes west of the city." She frowned. "Carly made the same mistake a little while ago. Do I act like a city girl?"

"Not even a little." He shook his head slowly. "Do you miss home?"

"I do."

∽

DAN OPENED the driver's side door, and Ashley quickly slipped out the passenger side before he could come around and open the door for her. The last thing they needed was to make this meeting any more like a date.

"I would've opened your door." He blinked several times.

"Do you want to sit over there?" She indicated a picnic table not far from the water.

"It might be chilly by the water. How about over there in that copse of trees, it offers shelter from the wind, but there's a great view of the lake?"

"Sounds ideal." She headed to the picnic table he'd indicated and sat down on the bench.

"Looks like most of the lake has frozen over." He pointed to a section of the lake. "It won't be much longer before the kids are out there playing ice hockey."

"I'm sure there will be figure skaters, too."

"Maybe a few, but they have to fight the hockey players for space."

"That isn't fair."

"It's simply the way it is."

She dug her notepad and pen out of her handbag.

He leaned toward her and placed a hand on her arm. "Do you want the restaurant to purchase a laptop for you?"

She shook her head. "Why would you do that?"

He dropped his hand. "It seems a necessary expenditure. Our head chef should have one."

"I can buy my own."

"I'll order one tomorrow. There is plenty of room in the budget for it."

"Carly needs it more than I do. She does most of the computer work. Get it for her instead."

"We'll order two." He smiled. "You know the two of you are welcome to give work to Sabrina. She's my administrative assistant, but she works for the Liberty Grille. Ask her. If she's not busy, she'll handle whatever you need."

"I would hate to bother her with my trivial stuff. As for the computer, if you think it's necessary than I'll take it."

"I'm sure your sample menus will be far more presentable when they're typed up."

"Fair enough." She looked down at her hands. "I tried to set up my desktop computer, but I'm missing the screen." She sighed. "I can't imagine how I lost it. Maybe it got left in the moving truck."

"You should be able to purchase a new screen in Freedom."

"I should buy a whole new computer. It's outdated anyway." She clicked her pen and poised it to write in her notebook. "What did you have in mind for your father's party?"

He laughed. "I hoped you'd have some ideas. I'm dreadful at that kind of thing."

"Tell me about your dad, and I'll see what I can come up with, but you might consider asking Haven. She's an event planner for a reason."

"Maybe I'll do that. You can at least help me narrow down the menu though, right?"

"Sure. Were you thinking sit-down or buffet?"

"Personally, I prefer buffet style, but Mother would never go for it, so it will need to be a formal sit-down meal."

"Do you want something simple like a choice between chicken and steak or something a little more elaborate?"

"I don't know. You pick."

"Dan, I don't even know your family. Help me out here."

"Chicken and steak are fine."

"We could do a simple salad with a raspberry vinaigrette dressing or we could do a caesar salad, or even a cobb salad, though that might be too filling. Do any of those sound appealing?"

"My mother would like the raspberry vinaigrette, I think."

"Maybe I should plan the menu with your mother." She let the sarcasm come across loud and clear.

ELLE E. KAY

"Excellent idea. I'll set up a meeting for you two for tomorrow after the lunch rush."

She set her pen and paper down. "I guess we're done here. Can you give me a lift back to the lodge?"

"I thought we were getting dinner?" He cocked his head to the side.

She shrugged. "Wasn't dinner for planning purposes?"

"Nah. I thought we could hang out tonight."

Her hands fluttered in front of her, so she folded them in her lap. "Okay." If she could get her heart to slow down, she could enjoy this time with her crush. Even though she didn't stand a chance with him, she wanted to spend every possible moment she could in his presence.

~

DAN AND Ashley entered Valentino's, and he inhaled the scent of fresh dough and Italian spices. It felt like coming home. It was his favorite place to unwind and had been since he was a teenager.

"Why don't you find us a seat, and I'll order." He strolled up to the counter and ordered their pizza. When he got to the table she'd chosen, he grinned. It was the seat he chose whenever it was available, and she even left him the side of the booth with a clear view of the door. There was something about Ashley. She seemed to know him on a deeper level than any of his previous girlfriends. Why couldn't he stop thinking of her in that light? She was a friend and an employee. Nothing more. For some reason that bothered him more than it should.

He sat down across from her and handed her a bottle of

water.

"Thanks."

"You're welcome." He leaned back in the seat. "The food should be out in a minute."

"Excellent. I'm famished." She fidgeted with her napkin.

"You mentioned siblings, didn't you?"

"Yep. I'm a middle child. I have an older sister and a younger brother." She leaned back as the server set their pizza on a pedestal. "Thank you." She nodded at the server before looking back at Dan. "What about you? Do you have siblings?"

"I have an older sister." He put a slice of pizza on each of their plates.

"Why doesn't she come into the Liberty Grille?" She took a bite.

"She moved away. Married a man from Texas and relocated there. I visited her when I did my two-week drill at Fort Bliss around the time of your interview."

"The reason you were in uniform when you interviewed me?"

"That's correct."

"What's it like? Being in the military?" She leaned forward, and he got the sense that she cared.

"Reserves? It's a cake walk compared to active duty." He took a bite of pizza, but barely tasted it as his mind traveled back to the Middle East.

"Do you miss active duty?"

"I do at times. It's another world. When I'm focused on making sure the device in front of me doesn't explode, nothing else matters. It clears my head. Unfortunately, as I moved up in rank, it was more than just my life on the line."

"That sounds ominous. I sense a story behind it."

"Another time, perhaps."

"What do you do in the Reserves?"

"Since they didn't have my MOS in the Reserves, I had to go through AIT again."

"So you did something with explosives when you were active duty?"

"I was a Ranger, but my MOS was 89 Delta."

"What's that?"

"Explosive Ordinance Disposal."

"Sounds dangerous."

"It is." A muscle jumped in his jaw, and his mouth went dry, so he guzzled his water. If he didn't steer this conversation away from his time in Afghanistan, he might share more than he was ready to divulge. "When I enlisted in the reserves, I decided on 68 Sierra. I didn't know what I wanted to do, and it was one of the few jobs that came with a substantial bonus, so I picked it. My title is Preventative Medical Specialist, but it basically amounts to what civilians would call infection control."

"That sounds interesting."

"It's not. They don't give me much to do on my weekend assignments. They usually stick me with the medics. Since Reserve units can be called active at any time, we need to have every position filled. Normally, there isn't much need for infection control on our base, but if we are ever activated, my position will be essential."

She nodded her understanding and took a sip of her water.

"When I was at Annual Training this year, I actually used my skills. I had to put in paperwork to shut down a food truck. Their regular guy inspected the same truck the week before, and they didn't get it up to snuff before my inspection. The Colonel had the Post Commander sign off and they lost their license to operate on base. I hated to turn that paperwork in, but I couldn't turn a blind eye on unsafe food practices."

"Unsafe food practices are a bad thing. I learned all about that in culinary school. I can see how your military job relates to your civilian job." Her eyes twinkled. "I didn't even know the Army had positions like that. My dad was in the Army, but I don't know much about what he did."

"He was too young for Vietnam, I imagine."

"Much. He was in the first gulf war. After that he was stationed in Germany for a while and brought us with him, but it was only for a couple of years when I was young. I don't remember anything about it."

"Did you ever consider joining the military?"

"No." She shook her head. "My parents were clear about what I was to do and that was go to college and get a 'respectable degree.'" She added emphasis with air quotes. "They were livid when I chose culinary school. If I had enlisted in the military, I think my father's head would've exploded."

"What about your mother?"

"She goes along with whatever my father wants. She prefers not to make waves."

"She doesn't sound anything like my mother. She's the complete opposite. You'll meet her tomorrow. I'll warn you she can be a bit snobbish. She was a New York socialite vacationing in Vail when my father swept her off her feet. I don't think she ever imagined herself living in a small town in backwoods Colorado, but she adjusted for the most part. My father is a developer who develops properties all over the country, so he could've chosen to live anywhere, but he was born and raised in Freedom and wasn't willing to leave."

"I'm sure your mom is lovely."

"Wait until after you meet Mother to form an opinion." He chuckled. "She's not an easy woman to get along with."

SEAN GLANCED at his watch and set down the bouquet of flowers he'd picked up in town. He had a date with his new girlfriend, but she'd have to wait. He sent a text telling her he was tied up with work.

He planned to follow Ivy to see if she followed through on the instructions he'd given her. This time, soldier boy would know he had a nemesis. A worthy opponent who would make him pay for his mistakes. Ivy shared the story about the Helmand Province and the dead soldiers, but that wasn't his concern. Winchester was responsible for destroying his life, and for that he would suffer.

When Ivy got into her Mustang, he put his Dodge Challenger in drive and followed careful to leave a few car lengths so she wouldn't know he was behind her. As he suspected she led him to his target. How she'd known Winchester would be at Valentino's he couldn't guess, but she sashayed in like she owned the place.

He watched through the window until she was seated, then followed her inside and studied the menu. Once he'd ordered, he made eye contact with Winchester, and the Army boy had the gall to grin at him. Maybe ruining lives was a game to him, but he'd soon find out what it was like to have everything you cared about taken from you. He stared at Ivy long enough to be sure she'd see he was watching her. She lowered her gaze to her water bottle. The woman didn't appear to have malice on her mind. He might need to be more persuasive.

The man behind the counter handed him his pizza in a box, and he strolled out of the restaurant.

It wasn't long before Ivy ambled back out to the parking lot, got into her Mustang and drove off, but it seemed to take an inordinate amount of time for soldier boy to finish eating with his little girlfriend. When he finally exited the establishment, forty-five minutes had passed.

He stayed behind them making sure to leave extra car lengths to keep them from noticing him.

Winchester came to a stop at the lodge, dropped his girl at her car, parked, and headed inside. In that moment, Sean was left with the choice of whether to follow the girlfriend, go inside and meet his date, or wait for Winchester.

It was possible he could follow her home and make it back before his target left the lodge, but if he did, he'd miss out on getting some sugar.

He parked and sauntered into the lodge. His girl was nowhere to be found when he entered the lobby, so he wandered over to Mountain Mug and ordered himself a Pumpkin latte with extra sugar and got her a White Chocolate Almond Avalanche since she'd mentioned it was her favorite.

His girl came out of the restaurant and spotted him. She frowned. "I'm sorry. Have you been waiting long? When you said you were tied up with work, I thought I'd have a little longer to help clean up the kitchen."

"Don't you have staff for that kind of thing?"

"We do, but I don't mind helping."

"That's adorable." He handed her the latte and took a sip of his own. "You look beautiful, sweetie."

"Thanks, Sean."

"Shall we go?" He held out a hand, and she placed hers in it. "What would you like to do tonight?"

"Valentino's is open late on Friday nights and I haven't eaten. Do you mind if we go there?"

He didn't want to disappoint her, so back to the pizza joint it was. Hopefully, she wouldn't notice the untouched pizza sitting in the backseat. "If that's what you want, that's where we'll go."

5

Ashley glanced down at the notebook in her lap. It was strange sitting at the round table in Dan's office without him present, but he'd asked her to wait there for his mother. Mrs. Winchester was due to arrive soon, but Ashley didn't feel prepared. Despite meeting with Haven and getting her thoughts and ideas for the event, and coordinating the menu to work with everything else, she was certain nothing she chose would be adequate. She wished she hadn't agreed to this meeting. Dan had taken seriously her sarcastic remark about meeting with his mother and made it a reality. She looked down at her shaking hands and forced them to still. It was a lesson for sure. She would do her best to avoid sarcasm in the future.

Dan's office door swung open, and her heart sped up when she saw his handsome face. His arm was around a thin woman she assumed was his mom. She wore an ivory pantsuit and had pearls at her neck. Her perfectly coiffed dark brown hair was elegant in a french twist.

"Mom, I'd like you to meet our head chef, Ashley."

"A female head chef. Way to go, Ashley."

She felt heat rise to her face as she rose to shake the other woman's hand. "It's nice to meet you, Mrs. Winchester."

"It's a delight to meet you. Daniel mentioned that you thought it would be beneficial to meet with me instead of him to plan the menu."

Ashley sent the man in question a sideways glare before returning her attention to his mom. "I have a few ideas we can go over. I met with the event planner to see what she had in mind for the party and designed three menus that I think would work well for a formal sit-down meal."

Mrs. Winchester skimmed the page Ashley handed her. "This will be easier than I thought. Thank you for being so prepared." After reading through the options, she smiled. "Menu three is glorious. I love the choice of mushroom asiago chicken or hickory bourbon glazed salmon, but can we substitute the garbanzo-stuffed mini peppers from menu one. Daniel's father is allergic to shellfish, so I don't think the crab crescents are a great idea."

Ashley gave Dan a blistering look before turning back to his mom. "Dan neglected to mention that detail."

Mrs. Winchester cringed. "Daniel is such a beautiful name, but for some reason he insists on letting people call him Dan or Danny. Such a shame."

"Sorry about that. I didn't realize you didn't like it, but I wholeheartedly agree that Daniel sounds much better than Dan."

The woman's smile was genuine. "I think we're going to get along brilliantly. It was wonderful to meet you, Ashley." She turned to her son. "Why don't you take me to meet your event planner now?"

"I didn't make an appointment with Haven, so I'll have to buzz her and see if she has time to meet."

Ashley made her way to the door. "If that's all, I'm going to get back to work?"

"Great. Thanks, Ash."

"You're welcome, Daniel." She drew out his name. She could hear his laugh as she closed his office door.

~

DAN GLANCED at his watch. It was about time to make rounds through the dining room and ask the diners if they were enjoying their meals. If he cut through the kitchen on his way back to his office, he might have a chance to say hello to Ashley. It'd been a busy evening, so he hadn't seen her in hours. She would need a break by now, he'd check and see if she could get away from the kitchen for a short break. Taking the hall that led directly into the dining room and bypassing the kitchen he roamed from table to table greeting locals and tourists alike. It was mostly locals, but in another week the season would pick up and the tourists would descend on their mountain paradise.

As he neared the massive stone fireplace he spotted Mayor Starling and his wife sitting in their favorite spot. He grinned and approached their table. "I'm looking forward to the parade, I hear this year will be better than ever."

Mrs. Starling sat up straighter. "You betcha. We have exciting plans. The highlight of the night will be the little ballerinas from Miss Cat's dance class though. Just you wait until you see those precious angels."

"I'm sure they'll be adorable as always."

Mayor Starling cleared his throat. "We do have some wonderful plans for this year's parade, but let's not get ahead of ourselves. We still have the tree lighting ceremony coming up. I was wondering if you'd be open to playing your guitar and singing?"

"I don't know about that. It's our busiest time of year." The excuse was plausible. How could he tell them he didn't want to sing songs glorifying God when he felt like God abandoned him?

"Nonsense." Mrs. Starling patted his hand. "We're counting on you. Don't let us down, Danny."

He left their table in no mood to continue his rounds, but duty called, so he stopped at each and every table until he made it past the bar and arrived at the entrance to the kitchen. None of the guests had complaints and many raved about the food and service. Nights like that were rare, so he intended to take full advantage.

After pushing through the double doors, he was greeted by the noise of clattering dishes and loud voices shouting over each other. The aroma of pumpkin spice lingered in the air. He glanced around to identify the source and his mouth watered at the sight of pumpkin rolls. Van sprinkled confectioner's sugar over top of them before sliding them into the chiller.

Dan pulled his attention from the dessert and scanned the kitchen until his eyes landed on Ashley. She was giving orders like a drill sergeant. He chuckled to himself. It was the part of the job he'd been worried she wouldn't be competent enough to handle. She was a pro. As mousy and timid as she was outside of the restaurant, she was the opposite in the kitchen. Her Southern Gospel played in the background as she took charge of the kitchen staff. Walking up behind her, he leaned down and whispered in her ear. "Have a minute?"

She spun around too quickly and lost her balance. He

reached out to steady her. The zing that traveled up his arm was unexpected.

"I'm sorry, Dan. You startled me."

"My apologies. I was wondering if you had time for a break."

"Sure." She walked over to Carly. "Would you take over for fifteen?"

"Will do." Carly grinned like the matchmaker she was. If it was up to her, he'd have been married off by now.

He led the way to the exit near his office and held the door for her.

"It's kind of a chilly night to be outside." Ashley said.

"True, but they've got the fires lit, so we can sneak over to the closest one and keep warm while we get some fresh air."

She shrugged and walked beside him. The peachy scent of her shampoo drifted his way as he made his way to one of the seating areas. The fire in the grate crackled, and Ashley held her hands up to it. She stared up at the sky. "I'll never tire of the stars up here. They're so beautiful."

"Don't you see them at home?"

"Not like this. Here it feels like I could reach out and touch them."

"I take the night sky for granted having grown up here."

"Probably the same way I take the Betsy Ross House and the Liberty Bell for granted."

He chuckled. "Yeah. Something like that."

Out of nowhere she punched him in the arm. Hard.

"What was that for?"

"Not telling me your father was allergic to shellfish. Did you want your mother to hate me?"

"I didn't think to mention it. We'd talked about steak and chicken, so I thought that was what you'd present to Mother. I had no idea that you would go to so much trouble coming up with three menu options complete with appetizers."

"You should've known that I'd be prepared."

He leaned down and tucked a stray hair that had escaped her bun behind her ear. "You're the same woman who presented the menu for ski season on a wrinkled-up piece of notebook paper."

"That was different. You and Carly were the only ones I thought would see it."

He reached for her hand. This was dangerous territory, and he knew it. One wrong move and their carefully constructed friendship would become something more complicated, but he couldn't help himself. His thumb made slow circles on her palm. "So, you're comfortable enough with me to let me see the real you?"

"We should get back." She snatched her hand back like she'd been burned, but her little intake of breath and the hooded look in her eyes betrayed her. She felt the chemistry between them even if she wasn't ready to admit it.

He followed her back inside but turned into his office instead of joining her in the kitchen. The sound of Ashley's blasted music reminded him why a relationship with her was out of the question. Tomorrow morning she'd be at Freedom Bible Church worshiping the Lord with a heart full of joy. He couldn't share her faith. Not anymore. He had no intention of entering a church again. Any romantic notions he had toward his head chef needed to be quashed.

~

DAN PULLED up outside of Ashley's house. Haven had called him when she couldn't get a hold of Kevin, the lodge manager. The truck carrying the Christmas trees they'd ordered for the lodge had overturned on the highway, so the trees wouldn't be arriving as scheduled. Thankfully, nobody was injured in the accident.

Instead of stressing over losing their choice trees. He told Haven he'd do his best to remedy the situation. He'd called Ashley to see if she wanted to visit Evergreen Ranch. They would pick out a couple of trees for the banquet rooms and see if they could find one for the main lobby. If the tree farm had one that would work, he'd find out if Haven wanted to come look or ask Mr. Harrington or Kevin to give final approval to have it delivered.

He hurried up Ashley's stairs and knocked on her front door.

"Come on in." Ashley ushered him in and the smell of apples and cinnamon greeted him. "There are muffins on the counter. Help yourself. I need to grab my coat, and then we can go."

"I see you still haven't finished unpacking." He eyed the tabby who had once again fixed her gaze on him from her perch atop the pile of boxes.

"I haven't had time." She grinned. "I'm looking forward to picking out the trees. This will be fun."

"Haven't you been to a tree farm before?"

"No. We've always had an artificial tree."

"That's terrible!"

"It wasn't so bad."

"Nothing beats the smell of a real Christmas tree."

"Not everyone has that luxury."

He drove onto the ranch road and down one of the lanes between the trees. "Let's see what we can find, shall we?"

When he opened the passenger door, she bounced out of her seat, not bothering to hide her giddy excitement. He savored the moment. This was a first for her, and they would experience it together. He picked up a fallen twig and broke some needles in half inhaling the fresh pine before handing the twig to Ashley, so she could do the same. There were other local Christmas traditions he could share with her. A plan began to form. This year he would share his Colorado Christmas with the tiny blond beside him.

"What do you think of this one?" Ashley stared up at a tree that was probably more than ten feet high. He stood beside it. "Look up, Ash. I'm 6'3" and that tree towers over me."

"Oh."

"I don't think we'll want to wrestle that beast into the banquet rooms, and it won't fit in my truck bed either. Let's stick to a tree under seven feet tall, okay?" He smiled. "But you can look for a fourteen- or fifteen-foot tree for the lobby of the resort if you'd like."

She skipped around looking for one and stopped at a gorgeous douglas fir that was the perfect height. "How's this?"

"I think Mr. Harrington will love it. Let's get someone to hold it for us until he or Kevin can get out here to look at it."

They found the owners of the tree lot and explained about the accident involving their ordered trees. The Evergreen Ranch owners, Candy and Chris, were thrilled at the prospect of getting the lodge's business.

When their discussion with the owners wrapped up, he pulled Ashley back into the line of trees. She immersed herself in the tree picking experience once again. "How about this one?" She stood by a tree around his height, so he deemed it acceptable.

"It'll work." He pointed out another tree standing nearby. "That one will do for the other banquet room."

"Excellent choice." Her cheeks had a rosy glow from the cold.

His gaze fell to her lips. It would be so easy to get carried away in the excitement of the holidays and pull her to him. Instead, he knelt down and sawed the base of the first tree. A few minutes later, he was carrying one of the two trees to his truck. Once both trees were loaded, they drove back to the front, and he hurried inside to pay for their purchases and return the saw.

On his way into the building, he stopped to admire some wreaths with beautiful bows on them. Ashley's place wasn't decorated, so he thought she might appreciate the gesture. He picked out a favorite and took it with him to the counter along with an over-the-door hook.

Back at the truck, he tossed the wreath into the back. "We've got to make a quick stop, okay?"

"Sure."

She looked confused when he pulled up outside of her house. He got out of the truck, and she followed suit. He lifted the wreath from the bed of his truck and held it out to her. "I thought this might help you enjoy Christmas more."

"Thank you. That was so thoughtful of you." Standing on her tiptoes, she kissed his cheek. It took every ounce of self-restraint he could muster to keep from pulling her close and kissing her lips. He searched her eyes and was sure she felt the same attraction. Would she respond to his kiss or would she push him away? Today wasn't the day to find out.

She unlocked her front door, and he hung the wreath for her. The drive back to the lodge passed in comfortable silence.

Dan delivered the Christmas trees into the banquet rooms, and once they were set up, he left the decorating in Haven's capable hands.

AFTER THEIR Evergreen Ranch excursion Ashley stopped in the kitchen to make sure her ingredients were ready for the first big week of the season. She wouldn't want to disappoint the guests expecting a scrumptious meal. Once she was certain everything was in order, she said her goodbyes to the kitchen staff and went searching for Dan to see if he was ready to leave.

The discordant fragrances of pine resin and heady perfume greeted her when she entered the banquet room. Dan stood in the corner and Ivy clung to him like a barnacle to a side of a ship. She backed out of the room.

What a fool she was. She never should've allowed herself to believe they had a special connection. She'd known from the start that she couldn't compete with Ivy.

Casey would be getting off her shift at the Mountain Mug,

so she could ask her for a ride home. Approaching the counter she placed an order with Ty, the evening barista.

Casey removed her apron and came around the counter. "Hi Ash! It's not like you to stop in on your day off."

"I was hoping to ask a favor, Case."

"Sure thing."

"Dan drove me in earlier, but he's preoccupied. If you're heading home, I was hoping to catch a ride with you."

"Certainly. I'm going that way, anyhow."

Ashley held the peppermint peaks mocha latte in her bare hands hoping to absorb some of its warmth through her skin. She'd left her gloves in Dan's truck. She hopped up into Casey's jeep and took in the picturesque view of mountain peaks as far as the eye could see. Snow swirled around them like they were stuck inside a snow globe. Her surroundings warred with her turbulent emotions.

"I'm glad I have four-wheel drive. You ought to think about getting a truck or jeep yourself."

"The car I drive is all-wheel drive."

"That'll do unless it gets deep. Then you might need to call Danny for a ride to work."

"Maybe I should look into trading in my car for a truck."

"It isn't that often that the roads are impassable, but I find it advantageous to have a reliable snow-worthy vehicle."

Casey pulled up in front of her house and Ashley suddenly realized she hadn't given the other woman directions. "How did you know where I lived?"

"Easy. You moved into the house my ex-boyfriend vacated, and my mom was your real-estate agent."

"Margie is your mother?" At Casey's nod, Ashley laughed. "Small towns are something else."

"You'll love it here. Give it time."

"I'll take your word for it."

6

Dan groaned when he glanced at the clock on his bedside table. Why hadn't he heard his alarm? He reached for his cell to see if it was set, and saw it was flipped to the off position. Strange. He rarely turned it off and didn't remember doing so. So much for his detour into the spare room for a weight-lifting session. There wouldn't be time today.

He hurried into the bathroom, ran a comb through his hair, and brushed his teeth. When he reentered his bedroom, his cell was ringing, but by the time he reached it he'd missed the call. Glancing at the caller ID told him it'd been his sister. He'd have to call her later. Oversleeping had put him way behind schedule, and he was supposed to be there to meet the new hire and introduce him to Ashley.

He threw on clothes and hurried out the door. The cold crisp morning held the promise of more snow on top of the two inches they'd gotten the day before, but it hadn't yet arrived. His grumbling stomach reminded him that he hadn't taken the time to eat. He'd have to grab a muffin at the Mountain Mug. After locking the door he turned toward his truck, but it wasn't there. He was certain he'd parked it in his usual spot in the driveway, but it was gone. He hit the remote on his key fob and heard the beep inside his garage. He hadn't put it there. He'd been expecting snow, but not enough to have to shovel out his vehicle which was the only time he used his garage for parking.

His spine stiffened, and he strode back into the house. The situation was suspect and didn't sit right. He used the man door to enter his garage since he couldn't open it from the outside without his remote opener. His EOD and Army Ranger training kicked in, and he checked under his vehicle to make sure a device hadn't been planted. After a thorough inspection, he got in his truck and backed out of the garage.

The events of the past week made real the possibility that he was losing his mind.

A LOUD BANGING on the kitchen door got Ashley's attention, so she investigated the ruckus and discovered a young man in a letterman's jacket knocking on the metal door. She pushed open the creaky door. "May I help you with something?" It was a door only used for deliveries, but he didn't seem to have a truck.

"I'm Thomas."

"Hi, Thomas. What can I do for you?"

"I was told to be here at ten o'clock."

"Who were you told to see?'

The kid pulled a note from his pocket. "Daniel Winchester or Ashley Castle."

"That would be me. The Ashley Castle part, I mean. I wasn't expecting you, but come in, and I'll see if I can help you."

"I'm the new junior chef."

"Oh." One corner of her mouth lifted. "Welcome aboard. I'll help you get settled. Carly will be here shortly. You'll shadow her your first day, and she'll decide when you're ready for more."

He followed her through the kitchen and out to the back hallway. She pointed out the locker room and then showed him the rear door. "In the future, you'll want to use this door. It's closer to the staff parking and it's usually unlocked.

THE RIDE into work was uneventful. When he arrived Ashley was showing Thomas around the kitchen.

"Ash?"

She turned to face him. "Yeah?"

"I'm sorry."

"About?"

"Can we speak in private?"

"Of course." She turned and gave Thomas a huge grin, and a stab of jealousy hit him. The idea of Ashley with the kid was preposterous. There was nothing to be envious about. Ashley couldn't be interested in the young buck, and even if she was, it didn't matter. She didn't belong to him, so it wasn't his concern. "I need to go meet with the boss. I'll be back in a few minutes. In the interim, you can get ready. There are aprons in the locker room."

It didn't normally bother him when she called him 'boss,' but something about the way she'd emphasized the word annoyed him.

Once she entered his office, he followed and shut the door behind him aware that he was scowling, but unable to school his features into a kinder expression.

"Is something wrong, boss?" She tilted her head to the side.

"Already flirting with the new help, I see." He shoved his hands in his pockets. "That didn't take long."

"What are you talking about?"

"Don't act naive, you knew what you were doing."

"That's absurd. You're crazy. He's barely more than a child." Color rose to her cheeks, and she crossed her arms over her chest.

"I apologize for not being here to meet him. My alarm got turned off and messed up my whole morning routine."

"Is that why you're cranky?"

"I'm not."

She stared at him a moment and lifted an eyebrow.

"Maybe a little. Sorry if I misread that back there, but we can't have employees dating. It'll cause problems."

"You don't have to worry about me."

"Why? Are you seeing someone?"

"No. Not that it's any of your business."

"Where did you disappear to yesterday? I looked for you, but you were gone. I thought I was driving you home."

"I wasn't feeling well, so I asked Casey to take me home."

"Are you feeling better now?"

"Sure. I'm fine."

"Good."

"The laptops came in this morning. Sabrina will give them to you. If you need assistance getting them set up, you can call IT."

"Okay."

"Meanwhile, get the new menu to Sabrina, so she can type it up and get the insert printouts ordered. We're running out of time."

She shook her head. "I gave you the menu."

"You didn't keep a copy?"

"I didn't know I would need it again."

"Fine. I'll make sure she gets it." He sat down at his desk and turned on his computer. "In the future, if you can't type something up yourself, give it to Sabrina so she can before it gets to me."

He needed to have a chat with her about her professionalism. What would possess her to turn in a hand-written menu scratched out and scribbled over without even bothering to make herself a copy. And why hadn't it bothered him at the time? "You may go."

ASHLEY FOUGHT tears as she stood outside of Dan's office and focused on her breathing. What had happened? The day before, Dan had been his usual charming self. He'd been sweet and kind and had even flirted with her, but today he was completely different. She wiped away the tears she could no longer control and wondered what she'd done to turn him against her?

She was certain she hadn't been coming on to Thomas, but even if she had flirted with the kid, Dan was with Ivy, so what was his problem?

She wasn't interested in the newly arrived junior chef. There was only one man at the lodge who captivated her attention, and he'd made it crystal clear that workplace romances were off-limits. He must've carved out an exemption for ex-fiancées, so he could continue to date Ivy.

Slowly, she started down the hall back to the kitchen, but stopped when she heard Ivy's voice coming from the locker room. She'd arrived earlier than usual.

"I did as you asked. I want my payment," Ivy said.

"You'll get paid after you complete the job."

"You wanted to frighten him, and now he's scared. What more do you want?"

"You think a few little changes around his house are going to bother him? No. We need to go big. Make his life flat-out miserable. I'll give you a down-payment, but I expect you to up your game. Seriously, you put his truck in his garage? That's your big move?"

Ashley tucked into the kitchen out of sight when she heard footsteps coming her way. What on earth had Ivy gotten herself into? It seemed dangerous. Who was the 'he' she was supposed to scare? Could they be referring to Dan? Was Ivy using him? Maybe she should tell him what she'd heard.

No. That would be a colossal waste of time given his current mood. Besides, he'd certainly take Ivy's word over hers, and she'd find herself jobless in Freedom, Colorado. She splashed cold water on her face and slogged back into the kitchen.

"I didn't know Danny-boy hired us a stud." Carly winked at the young man standing beside her. "He's going to teach me everything he learned in school."

"And you'll teach him everything you learned on the job, huh?" Ashley moved to the sink and washed her hands.

"Something like that."

"We need to get to work. The lunch crowd won't wait for us to finish gabbing."

"Something wrong, Ashley?"

"Nope."

"Your face begs to differ." Carly stirred the flour and seasoning mixture in her bowl with extra gusto until some flew out of the bowl.

"Watch it. I don't need Dan calling me into his office again."

"Ah. And now we know what's got you down." Carly frowned. "What did he call you in for?"

"To apologize for not being here to greet Tom."

"That doesn't sound so bad."

Ashley didn't respond. Carly hadn't been there, so she had no idea how awkward their discussion had been. She stepped into the walk-in refrigerator and began gathering ingredients. It was normally something others handled for her, but she needed a moment to cool off after her encounter with Dan and the strange conversation she'd overheard.

ELLE E. KAY

AT THE KNOCK on his office door, Dan sat up straighter. He'd been hunched over his desk going cross-eyed from staring at the prior week's receipts. "Come in."

"Did you need anything before I go, boss?" Ashley leaned against his door frame. "I'm getting ready to head out so I can make it to midweek prayer service."

"Are we all set for Saturday's banquet?"

"We are." She gave him a tight smile. "When does your sister fly in?"

"Friday morning."

"Are you picking her up at Denver International?"

"I offered, but Beth didn't want me to drive that far when she could just as easily rent a car."

"Makes sense." She rubbed the back of her neck. "You sure there isn't anything you need before I go?"

What he needed was to restore his friendship with her, but that couldn't be done before she left for service. He glanced at his watch. "No. You go ahead. Have fun."

His gaze remained on her until she closed the door behind her. She'd seemed distant all week, and he couldn't figure out what he'd done to deserve her cold shoulder. He hadn't handled it well when he'd thought she was flirting with Thomas, but it seemed like there was something more between them than one awkward conversation.

Since he was unable to focus on the numbers in front of him any longer, he tossed them into a file, put the file in his desk drawer, and locked it. Tomorrow was a new day; he'd finish it then. He straightened his tie and grabbed his suit jacket. A stroll through the dining room to check on their customers might improve his mood.

An hour later, he said goodnight to Carly and Thomas and headed out. If he couldn't concentrate after a few minutes in Ashley's presence, how was he going to be on Saturday. The two of them needed to hash out whatever it was that was bothering her. In the meantime, he had somewhere to go.

THE SMELLS of wet dog and disinfectant warred with each other as Dan opened the door of the local shelter. He followed the shelter volunteer, and she took him to meet the dogs. Though many of them were intelligent and affectionate, a husky mix won him over. Something about his expressive blue eyes, and the way he leaned against Dan's leg as if they were best friends already made it impossible to pass him over.

Once he signed the adoption papers and payed the fee, he headed to the store to grab a bag of dog food, new leash and collar, bowls and a bed.

Back at home, he sat down on the floor and played with his new furry friend. He sunk his fingers into the dog's thick fur and tried to come up with a name that fit the canine. "I think you look like a Sammy?"

The dog didn't bark or growl, so he settled on Sammy for his name.

When the house phone rang interrupting their playtime, he rose to answer it. "Hello?"

"Daniel, how are things going for Saturday?"

"Everything is fine, Mother." He sank onto the couch and

resumed petting Sammy.

"And what about you? Are you seeing anyone?"

"No, mother. I'm happily single. In fact, I adopted a dog to keep me company."

"How are you going to take care of a dog? You're never home." Indignation came across in his mother's voice.

He sighed. "I suppose I'll be forced to spend more time at home now that I have a reason to be here."

"You should concern yourself with finding a wife instead of adopting a dog."

"The dog is here now, and Sammy's staying."

"Sammy? That's a silly name for a dog."

"I like it. He looks like a Sammy."

"Your father is calling. I've got to go. I'll see you on Saturday."

"Goodbye, Mother."

7

Ashley was still mortified after seeing Dan with Ivy on Sunday, and Dan's berating her the following day hadn't helped.

She shouldn't have allowed herself to hope their friendship would turn into anything more. Besides, like she kept telling Carly, Dan was way out of her league. He was gorgeous, and she was average at best, but sometimes when he looked at her, she believed he felt what she did.

Today she needed to put him out of her head and do her job to the best of her abilities.

Ashley met with her kitchen staff and reminded them of Mr. Winchester's shellfish allergy. They served shrimp and crab-cakes in the main dining room, so they needed to take precautions to avoid cross-contamination. Of course, those precautions were standard, but it wouldn't hurt to remind everyone to act with extra diligence. Once everyone was given their assignments, she hurried down the hall to check the banquet room and make sure everything was ready.

The room was elegant. The tables were lain with white linen tablecloths and indigo napkins. The tree in the corner was decorated tastefully with scarlet bows, blue and white ornaments, and snowflakes. It added the perfect amount of festive spirit to the room. Once the guests arrived, the waitstaff would serve the hor d'oeuvres. Since it was a surprise party, they were allowing forty-five minutes before the first course was served.

She turned to leave the room and collided with Dan. "Sorry."

"You make a habit of running into me." He chuckled.

"I do, don't I?"

He shuffled his feet and glanced over at the banquet room. "How's it look inside?"

"Perfect. Haven did a lovely job."

"Excellent. The guests will begin arriving in a few minutes, so I'm going to wait at the front entrance of the lodge to greet them, and I'll have Amanda show them to the banquet room. My parents will arrive thirty minutes after the scheduled start time. That should leave ample time for the guests to arrive, so they can shout 'surprise.'"

"Everything seems to be running smoothly. I'll be in the kitchen making sure everything stays on schedule."

"Thanks for everything, Ash." There was a twinkle in his eye when he said the words. "You're a dependable friend." There was that word again. She couldn't escape it. A *friend* was all she'd ever be to him.

"You're welcome. Glad I could help."

DAN STOOD at the door of the lodge and greeted his family and his father's friends as they arrived. There were discreet signs directing the way, but he preferred to spend the first few minutes of every event at the front door, so he could assist the guests himself. Considering this function was for his father, he felt even more obliged to do so.

He glanced at Amanda. The tall blond hostess chatted with Casey at the Mountain Mug while awaiting the guests' arrival. She'd seemed put out when he'd first requested she work on her day off, but when he brought up the overtime pay, she lost the attitude and happily worked the extra shift.

Ivy came through the door from the dining room into the lobby at the same time as he glimpsed his aunt and uncle. He glanced over at her and opened the front door for his relatives. He'd scheduled Ivy to work the main dining room so he could keep her away from his family. Greeting guests took longer than expected and before he knew it, his mother was texting him that they'd parked and were on their way inside. He hurried into the banquet room and let everyone know that his father was on his way in.

His dad acted surprised, but Dan believed he'd known about the party. It was hard to keep secrets from him.

The food was splendid, and everyone raved about it. By the time, the assortment of cheesecakes made their way into the room, most of the guests were stuffed, but few were able to resist the scrumptious desserts prepared by Chef Van Anderson. Their dessert chef was in a class of his own. Dan questioned why they hadn't lost him to one of the big city restaurants, but he wasn't complaining. Van was a loyal friend, and his masterpieces were delectable.

The crowd began to disperse, and Dan drifted from the dessert table over to the head table where his father stood beside his chair looking out over the emptying room. "Did you enjoy your party?"

"It was a huge success, son." His father clapped him on the back. "Thanks for your hard work."

"Anytime. Glad you enjoyed your birthday."

His father took a sip of water and set his glass back down.

Dan lifted his own water to take a sip, but set his glass down when he noticed his father's face and neck were turning red. His dad loosened his tie and sunk into a chair.

"What's wrong, Dad?"

His father's face contorted in pain. When he realized his dad couldn't speak, he dialed 911. He'd learned basic medical care in his training but hoped if his father needed treatment the paramedics would take care of it.

Heath, the security guard, came through the door. "I heard the call on dispatch." He gestured to the man who came in with him who was rolling up his sleeves and putting on a pair of latex gloves. "This here is Dr. Errol Broderick. He's a thoracic surgeon here on vacation. He agreed to provide assistance until the ambulance arrives."

Dr. Broderick met Dan's gaze. "He's flushing." He flashed a light down his throat. "Anaphylaxis. Does he have any known allergies?"

"Shellfish, but the menu was carefully crafted to avoid it."

"Then there was cross-contamination somehow." He pulled items from his bag. "Does he have an EpiPen?"

Dan looked to his mother, who shook her head. "I didn't think to bring it with us."

"Why don't you go outside and meet the ambulance? I'm

going to have to help him breathe."

Dan hurried to the front door of the lodge. The ambulance was pulling up when he got there. One of the EMTs introduced himself as Carson, and Dan showed him and his partner to the banquet room.

His mother ran up to him and clung to his arm. "Do you want to ride in the ambulance, Mother, or would you like me to drive you to the hospital?"

"I can drive myself." She sniffled.

"No. That's not a good idea. Your distraught. I'll drive you."

He followed a safe distance behind the ambulance with his mother ringing her hands in the passenger seat beside him.

***

ASHLEY HELPED the restaurant staff clear the banquet room. She kept Mr. Winchester's plate, glass, and flatware for testing. She didn't know how his food was contaminated, but she intended to do everything she could to find out. Once the items were bagged, she hurried to the security office to speak with Heath.

He was deep in conversation with Max Harrison, a police officer who frequently spent time at the lodge. When they spotted her, they stopped talking and motioned for her to join them.

"What can I do for you, Miss Ashley?" Heath asked.

She shifted her weight from one foot to the other and back again. "I have a strange request."

"What's that?"

"It's going to sound insane."

"Let's hear it."

"I'd like to know where I can have Mr. Winchester's glass and plate tested."

Officer Harrison scrunched his brows together. "Do you suspect foul play?"

"Honestly, yes." She sighed deeply. "Last Monday, I overheard a heated discussion, and although I can't be certain it was about Dan, every time it comes to mind, I can't help but think he was the one they argued about. The man wanted the woman to wreak havoc on his life."

"But this is Dan's father?"

"What better way to hurt a man than to go after his family?"

"You may have something there." Max reached for the plastic bag she held with the utensils, plates, and glass that Mr. Winchester used. "This is great, but if we're going to do this correctly, we need to test the rest of the dishes and utensils, as well. If it's on several items for different guests, we'll chalk it off to accidental cross-contamination. If, however, Mr. Winchester was the only one whose items were contaminated with the offending shellfish, we can safely assume it was intentional."

"I'd better hurry back then. The staff may have already started loading the dishes into the dishwasher."

"Heath, call down there and tell them to cease cleaning until I can get a crew in here."

"Consider it done." Heath said as he lifted his phone to his ear. A moment later he set down the phone. "Carly's got it covered. She's going to make sure nobody touches anything."

"Thanks for bringing this to our attention, Miss Castle. May I get your number in case I have further questions?"

"Of course." Heath handed her a notepad and pen, and she jotted it down, ripped off the top sheet, and gave it to Max.

"Is there any chance you know whose conversation you overheard?"

She sighed. "I don't want to get anybody in trouble unnecessarily."

"I'd say it's necessary at this point. Don't you think?"

"Yes, of course. You're right." She folded her arms over her chest. "I'm not sure who the man was, but the woman was Ivy Nelson. She's one of our waitresses."

"I know Ivy." He wrote down the name in a tiny notepad he pulled from his front pocket. "Thanks. I'll talk to her."

~

DAN PACED the waiting area at the hospital. He tried to ignore the pervasive odors of antiseptic, disease, and something he couldn't identify. A nurse had taken his mother back to see his father thirty minutes earlier, but he and Beth had been told to remain back.

Beth walked over to him and gave him a weak smile. "He'll be fine, you know?"

"Yeah. I know." He nodded.

"I'm going to go to the cafeteria and grab a coffee." Her eyes darted around the room before landing on him again. "Do you want anything?"

"Sure. I'll take a black coffee."

"Did you want to join me?"

"I'll wait here just in case."

"Okay. Call me if you hear anything before I get back."

His dad was out of the woods, but he felt responsible for the whole fiasco. Had he supervised the food preparation instead of trusting it to the kitchen staff, his father wouldn't have gone into anaphylaxis. He'd thought Ashley was competent, but she'd allowed this crisis to occur. Now, he was doubting his own judgment.

As the thought entered his mind, the object of his musing trudged in looking like she was the one needing a hospital bed.

She rushed to his side and placed a hand on his shoulder. "How is he?"

He could see the concern in her eyes, so he took a deep breath to keep himself from pulling away from her. Guilt was probably eating her alive, and while it wasn't his job to assuage it, he didn't want to make her suffer. "I'm not sure. They let my mother back, so I'm hopeful he's improving. My sister went down to the cafeteria to get some coffee."

"I don't even know what to say. This shouldn't have happened. Everybody was briefed on his allergy. We were extra diligent in the food preparation. I can't imagine how this could've happened, but it has to be my fault. The buck stops with me." Seeing the pained expression on her face made him realize she was nearly as devastated by the mishap as he was.

"No it doesn't, Ash. It stops with me. I'm the restaurant manager."

"With that logic, it would stop with Mr. Harrington since he's the lodge owner, but that's plain silly. I run the kitchen, so it's my fault."

"There is no advantage to arguing over whose fault it was, but we need to make sure this never happens again."

"On that point, we agree." Ashley sank down into a seat. He wondered if it was the first time she'd sat all day other than the drive to the hospital.

Beth returned with the coffees and handed him his cup and then turned her gaze on Ashley. "I'm sorry. I didn't know someone else was here, or I would've brought you one, too."

"I'm fine. Thanks."

"Beth, this is Ashley Castle. She's the head chef at the Liberty Grille."

Beth took Ashley's hand in hers and looked in her eyes. "Are you okay?" The compassion in his sister's eyes was almost too much for him to bear. She'd instantly recognized how hard Ashley was taking this and empathized with her instead of placing blame on her. He didn't know how to put his own feelings aside to comfort others the way she did.

Later that night after he finally convinced Ashley to go home, his sister approached him. "There is something more than a working relationship between you two. I sense it."

"We're friends. That's all."

"I'm not buying what you're selling." She shook her head vehemently. "You have feelings for that woman."

"Maybe, but I haven't explored them and I don't intend to do so."

"You're a fool."

"Why would you say that?"

"She's obviously smitten with you, and you have feelings for her, so why wouldn't you do something about it?"

~

DAN WALKED beside the nurse as she wheeled his father out of the hospital.

"I can walk. I'm not an invalid."

"I'm sorry, sir. It's policy."

"I don't care about—"

"Dad, let the nurse do her job. You wouldn't want to get her fired, would you?"

"No. I suppose not."

They exited the building at the main lobby. Dan left his father with the nurse and brought his truck around. He got out to help his dad get in on the passenger side, but he waved him away and got in on his own. After waving goodbye to the world's most patient nurse, Dan climbed back into the truck and drove to his parents' house.

Once they arrived, he and his father entered through the kitchen door. He sat at the breakfast bar and talked with his mother for a few minutes. She agreed to remain home and make certain his father followed doctor's orders and rested for the remainder of the day. His dad was already talking about going into work, so she would have her hands full with him.

"I'm going to head to the restaurant." Dan hugged his mother and waved to his dad who was comfortably resting in his recliner.

The drive to work was quiet, but his mind was anything but peaceful. What could've happened to allow such a mix-up in the kitchen? Was it an innocent mistake? Between it and the strange happenings at home, he wasn't so sure.

8

Thanksgiving at Liberty Grille was their busiest night so far this season. They'd been flooded with reservations over the last few days, so the wait was much longer than usual which meant the waitstaff was dealing with grumpy customers. Thankfully, the unhappy ones were offset by the customers exhibiting plenty of holiday spirit and gratitude. She'd heard several servers bragging about the excellent tips they'd received.

She was grateful that Dan had suggested a special menu for the holiday. The menu only included five options, and the majority of diners chose the traditional Thanksgiving feast. It made food preparation simpler and allowed them to keep the kitchen running smoothly behind the scenes.

Dan approached and she smiled. "Hey."

"How's it going?" He grinned. "I'm getting positive feedback on the food. The turkey is perfectly moist, the cranberries are delicious, and the sweet potato casserole is to die for."

Carly bowed. "Why thank you for sharing, boss. We try."

"Didn't anyone rave about my pecan pie?" Van asked.

"A few, but more were raving about the apple and pumpkin pies," Dan said.

"There is no accounting for taste." Van took several cake layers from the oven and set them down to cool.

Dan moved closer to Ashley and leaned in so only she would hear him. "Freedom's tree lighting is Sunday night, and since it's your night off, maybe we could go together?"

"You want to go with me?"

"I'd hate to go alone. I was hoping you'd join me."

"Sure. I'll go." She swallowed her disappointment. For a brief moment, she thought he was asking her out.

"Go where?" Carly asked.

"Dan and I are going to go to the tree lighting together as friends. We'd ask you to join us, but you're working."

"I'll catch up with you two after we close the restaurant."

"Sure." Dan smiled. "We'll see you there."

∞

ASHLEY HURRIED into her bedroom to get ready. She stood in front of her closet and stared at her options. She had no idea what clothing one wore to a tree lighting ceremony.

She reminded herself that it wasn't a date. Dan was taking her as a friend. She settled on a green sweater and black jeans. It was an outdoor event, so it should be appropriate attire.

The doorbell rang and she hurried to answer it, pulling on her dressy cranberry colored cashmere coat as she did.

"Hi there. You ready?" He smiled displaying his dimple.

"I am."

"You might want to grab a scarf and gloves. It'll get chilly tonight."

"Oh yeah. Give me one second." She rejoined him wearing a thick cable-knit scarf she'd knitted herself. "I left my gloves in your truck when we went to Evergreen Ranch."

"I forgot about that. I stuck them in the console. Don't you have another pair?"

She shook her head.

"Let's head out. You're going to love the Christmas tree lighting. It's a whole night of fun and festivities and serves as our official kickoff to the Christmas season."

A wind gust blew her scarf off one shoulder the moment she stepped out the door. Dan wrapped it around her neck and grinned as if to say 'I told you so.' He opened the passenger door for her, and she climbed into his truck.

He got in the driver's side and reached into his console and got her gloves for her.

"I'm surprised they don't need us at work."

"You always have Sundays off. Besides, it'll be a light crowd tonight since most of the tourists will be at the tree lighting with the locals."

"Glad to hear it. I'd hate to think I abandoned Carly to a packed restaurant."

"I wouldn't let that happen."

"You wouldn't, would you?"

"I try to be diligent when it comes to making sure all shifts are fully-staffed. It's a challenge at times when you find yourself unexpectedly short-staffed due to emergencies or call outs, but with Sabrina's help, we make-do."

"Let's forget about work for a while."

"Yes. Let's."

THEY BOTH turned their attention to Mayor and Mrs. Starling as they welcomed the town folk and tourists alike. The mayor announced that he'd asked Clifford Harrington, the owner of Freedom Ridge Resort to do the honors. He called Mr. Harrington up on stage, and the elderly gentleman hurried through the crowd. He walked with a cane, but it barely slowed him down. Once he was in place, Mayor Starling started the crowd in a countdown from ten. When they reached zero, Mr. Harrington flipped the switch and the tree glowed with blue and white lights. The crowd oohed and aahed. The mayor returned to the microphone. "Well, how about that?" The crowd applauded in response. "It's time to hang the ornaments on the tree. Let's form two lines, so we're not tripping over one another."

Dan nudged Ashley and pointed to the booth that looked like a little log cabin decorated with tiny white lights. "Want to go get a hot chocolate and some peppermint bark while the line is short?"

"Only if I can get some roasted chestnuts, too."

"You eat those?"

"They're delicious."

He grinned. "I'll buy you two bags of them."

She laughed. "One will do."

He purchased their hot chocolates and snacks, and they

found a bench from which to watch the festivities. The scent of hot chocolate mingled with the aroma of pumpkin and apples from nearby food vendors.

A few families smiled as they walked past, and envy pierced his heart. He'd thought he wanted what they had before, but Ivy's one-night stand with Gage had destroyed what he'd believed would be his happy-ever-after. He glanced down at the woman beside him and studied her as she watched children hanging ornaments on the tree. Would it be possible to have a forever with a girl like her? There was no way a godly woman like Ashley would give a prodigal like him a second glance. It would be best for him to keep his thoughts from veering from friendship into romance.

The Mayor made his way back up to the stage once the tree was filled with ornaments, and Dan took a deep breath knowing what was coming. He hoped he'd find the strength to get through it. He hadn't been able to say no to the mayor despite his desire to avoid singing. It wasn't in him to cause trouble by refusing a simple request. It would only be simple if God allowed him to get through the song despite his recent chilly attitude toward the Almighty. Maybe the Lord would choose that moment to strike him down, if so, he deserved whatever he had coming. Mayor Starling looked out over the crowd. "There you are, Danny. Come on up here."

"Would you excuse me for a few minutes? I'll be back after this."

"Of course," Ashley said.

He made his way up onto the stage and sat down at a stool with a microphone stand in front of it and picked up the guitar propped beside it.

"Please welcome Freedom's own Danny Winchester as he

ELLE E. KAY

sings us into the Christmas season."

The crowd went silent as the first strains of "O Holy Night" filled the sky. He sang with emotion and the gaping hole in his soul began to heal.

Fall on your knees, O hear the angel voices!

O night divine, O night when Christ was born!

The words he sang had an unexpected effect on him, but he wasn't sure where that left him and God. If he wanted the relationship restored, he knew it was up to him to return to the Lord.

Dan sought out Ashley once the mayor introduced the next performance. Her eyes met his and her smile melted him. As he descended the stairs, he knew he couldn't resist the golden-haired beauty who'd become important in every aspect of his life. She was the first person he called when he wanted to get out of the house and the first girl who came to mind when he considered dating again.

Questions swirled through his head. Would she be open to a relationship with him? What would she think when she learned what he'd done overseas? Would she be ashamed of him? He forced the questions and memories of failures and losses from his mind and held his hand out to Ashley. She allowed him to lace his fingers with hers and he walked her around introducing her to the locals.

When he spotted Aiden's mother who managed the local coffee shop, Stories and Scones, he placed his hand on the small of Ashley's back and guided her toward the woman. "Mrs. Clark it's wonderful to see you. You're looking lovely as usual. Nice touch with the fancy scarf."

"Oh, stop!" She fluffed the ends of her short hair and

made eye contact with Ashley. "This one's a real charmer. Watch out for him."

Ashley smiled. "I noticed."

Dan said, "I'd like you to meet Ashley Castle. She was hired on as Liberty Grille's head chef in September, so this will be her first winter at the lodge." He made eye contact with Ashley and then looked back to Mrs. Clark. "This is Aiden's mother, Jan Clark, she manages the town's coffee shop."

"Welcome to Freedom." Mrs. Clark smiled warmly. "You can call me Jan."

"Thank you, Jan. It's nice to meet you."

"Are you concerned about ski season?"

Ashley scrunched up her nose. "I'm a tad nervous, but we have a good manager at the Liberty Grille, so I'm sure everything will run smoothly." Her freckles stood out in the light from the streetlamp, and he couldn't help but admire her cute little upturned nose. There was no doubt left. He was falling for her. He shouldn't let himself do that.

Mrs. Clark smiled. "That's true. Danny's a good boy. I'm glad he found a nice girl to spend time with."

Dan nearly choked on his hot chocolate. "We're just friends."

"Sure you are." Mrs. Clark laughed.

"No. It's true. It's what Ashley wants."

"If you say so."

Ashley turned beat red. He put his arm around her shoulders and tucked her into his side so he could whisper into her ear. "I'm sorry. I didn't mean for her to misread our relationship." Putting his arm around her probably wasn't helping matters. Soon the whole town would think they were an item, but if it got other men to keep their distance, it might not be such a bad thing. She didn't pull away. Did that mean she felt something for him? Only time would tell.

~

ASHLEY HAD known she was infatuated with Daniel Winchester before hearing him sing the words of her favorite Christmas hymn, but in that moment, she lost her heart completely and knew there was no other man for her. She hadn't realized he was a believer, but nobody could sing that song with as much passion as he did without a heartfelt love of the Lord. It was an eye-opener for her.

She stared at his profile as he drove her home. The night had been one of the most enchanting nights of her life, and she didn't want it to end. When he stopped his truck outside of her house and walked her to the door, she pulled him down for a quick hug and kissed his cheek. "Thanks for tonight." She smiled. "I can't imagine a better way to start the Christmas season."

"I'm glad you came. I haven't had that much fun at a tree lighting ceremony in a long time. In fact, it's the first time I had that much fun." He took a deep breath. "I know we're supposed to be friends, but…"

"You don't have to say anything, Dan. I know you want to keep me in the friend-zone, and I understand." She reached for his hand and squeezed it before letting herself in her house and closing the door behind her. Why tears streamed down her face, she couldn't say. The night was perfect, but it was over, and she needed to bring herself back to reality. A reality that didn't include Daniel Winchester as her boyfriend. They'd had a nice time together out as friends. Ivy wasn't out of the picture, and even if she was, another girl like Ivy would take her place. Ashley would never be in the same league as Daniel.

Lord, help me to get over him. She sobbed softly and silently prayed. *I knew better than to let my heart get involved, but I'm a foolish girl. Give me wisdom and understanding, so I don't keep making the same mistakes.*

9

By 10:45 the mise en place was finished, and Ashley caught herself watching the door to the back hallway hoping Danny would walk through it. She mentally shook herself and turned to Carly who was working on her own food prep.

"Carly?"

"Yeah?"

"How come you never made it to the tree lighting last night?"

"Sean picked me up for our third date, and he said he wasn't interested in 'all that small-town rigmarole.'"

"I'm surprised you didn't ditch him and come anyway."

"I seriously considered it." Carly grinned. "How did your date go with Danny-boy?"

"It wasn't a date, but at times it sure felt like one." She closed her eyes thinking about the feel of his arm around her when he tucked her close to his side to whisper in her ear. "Hearing him sing was amazing."

"Danny sang? I haven't heard him sing since before he

was deployed."

Ashley lifted her eyes to Carly's, "I sure hope he doesn't wait that long before he sings again."

They both quieted when Dan came through the door. Ashley's stomach fluttered.

"You know ladies, I'm well aware that when the conversation stops when I enter a room, I was probably the topic of discussion."

"You were." Carly put a hand to her hip. "Why didn't you mention you were singing last night? You know I wouldn't have missed it."

He leaned his hip on the counter. "Because I didn't want to make a big deal out of it, and I knew you'd do just that."

"Ash?"

"Yeah?"

"My father's company is having a big Christmas event next Friday. He's pressuring me to attend, but I don't have a date."

"Why aren't you taking Ivy?" Ashley stared at the cumin to avoid meeting his eyes.

He lifted her chin with one finger. "Why would I take Ivy?"

She shrugged.

"I'd like to take you if you don't mind going as my plus one?"

"I'm on the schedule."

He looked over at Carly and lifted a brow.

Carly grinned. "We can switch shifts. It'll give me a chance to see how Thomas handles the Friday night pressure."

"Will that work?"

"I'd love to go with you."

Once he was out of earshot, Carly whispered, "So, do you still think you and Danny aren't dating?"

∽

DAN WATCHED as Carly and Ashley ambled across the parking lot, chatting as they walked. He waited until they reached Carly's car and hurled a snowball. It landed between the two ladies. Carly picked up some snow and firmed up a snowball which she threw at him. It hit him square in the chest. "You'll pay for that one, Carly."

She ducked into her car gave a little wave, backed out, and drove off.

"I will get her for that."

"I'm sure you will." Ashley laughed. "You did start it though."

"Have dinner with me?"

"It's a little late for dinner."

"I called ahead. Tori will be there."

"She took a reservation for ten o'clock at night."

"You wouldn't do that for a friend?"

"I suppose I would if I owned a restaurant, but I don't, so…"

He threaded their fingers together and started toward his truck.

"I should take my car, so I can drive home after."

"Nonsense. I'll bring you to work in the morning. I have to come in anyway, and I drive past your place."

The corner of her mouth lifted. "Okay. Lead the way."

Tori opened the door for them, and Dan entered Evelyn's with Ashley by his side. The mouth-watering smells of steak and seafood greeted them. Tori closed the door and disappeared into the back.

Despite the over-the-top Christmas decor, the atmosphere was romantic when he took his seat across from Ashley and watched her as she perused the menu. He knew her mind was analyzing the options the other restaurant served and wondering if Tori's dishes were as mouth-watering as her own.

"It's an honor to have Chef Castle in my restaurant." Tori said before she took their orders. "I let the waitstaff leave, so I'll be serving you myself tonight. Can I get your drink orders?"

"Sweet tea for me."

"I'll have the same," Ashley said.

Dan smiled. "Thanks for doing this, Tori. Ashley and I will return the favor when you're ready for a night out."

"You would do that for me?"

Ashley grinned. "I'd be happy to." She placed her hand on her chest. "This is my first time in your restaurant, it's lovely. I've heard amazing things about the food."

Tori grinned. "Likewise."

"If you two are done complimenting each other, I'm starved."

"Leave it to a man." Tori took out her pad to jot down their orders.

Ashley set down her menu. "I'll take the braised Colorado lamb shank, the California mix, and blue-cheese dressing on my salad."

Tori grinned. "Excellent choice."

Dan grunted. "I'll stick with the black Angus New York strip, a baked potato, and creamy Italian dressing on the salad."

"Why am I not surprised you ordered steak and potatoes?" Tori asked.

∞

THE FOOD was delicious, and the evening felt perfect. Ashley was nearly certain this was a date. Dan waited for Carly to leave before he'd asked her to join him for dinner, and he'd made reservations for two. Was someone else supposed to be here with him? Had Ivy canceled last minute, and he'd asked her to come as a replacement? She had so many questions, but she didn't have the courage to ask any of them. She wanted more than anything to let herself enjoy their time together. If she would stop analyzing their relationship, she could simply be with him and enjoy his company. That was proving impossible. She needed to know if he felt anything for her or if she was simply a friend as he'd insisted in the past.

The way he looked at her across the candlelit table wasn't the way he'd look at a friend. Was this the start of a romance? *Lord, please don't let me give him my heart if he's going to stomp on it.*

Dan reached across the table and took her hands in his. He leaned over and brushed her hair from her face. She thought for a moment that he was going to kiss her.

Tori came in with a chocolate mousse dessert, and it looked delicious. Dan smiled at her over the table. "I preordered dessert for us."

"I'm glad you did. I wouldn't have ordered dessert, but this looks scrumptious."

"Thanks for coming with me. I was hoping you wouldn't say no."

"When have I ever said no when you asked me to go somewhere with you?"

"You haven't, yet, but it doesn't keep me from thinking you will."

"That wouldn't make me a devoted friend, now would it?"

"About that—"

Tori came back and smiled. "I'm going to head out. You can leave out the back door and lock it on your way out. I left the spare key on the counter."

"Thanks again, Tori," Dan said.

"Take your time. There's no rush. We'll clean up in the morning."

"Looks like we have the place to ourselves." Dan made eye contact after they heard the door close.

"Alone with a man unsupervised. I don't think Pastor Stephenson would approve."

"I promise not to compromise your virtue, Ashley."

"Can I ask you something?"

"Of course."

"Why don't you go to church anymore?"

"God and I aren't on speaking terms."

"Care to elaborate?"

"Not tonight. Let's enjoy our evening."

When they finished their desserts, she carried the dishes back to the kitchen and turned on the sink.

"What are you doing?" Dan came up behind her.

"The dishes."

"Why?"

"I don't want Tori to come in tomorrow to a messy kitchen."

"I'll help you load them in the dishwasher, but you're not standing here hand washing dishes."

He took the plates and scraped them, and she turned on the faucet to rinse them. "I don't think Tori's commercial dishwasher requires prerinsing."

"No. I'm sure it doesn't." Ashley stared at the water as it ran across the plate.

"Why are we doing it?"

"I'm not sure." She giggled and squirted Dan with water. "You little brat." He wrestled the hose from her and put it back in its place. "I would've gotten even, but I don't want you to freeze when we get outside."

"I'm sorry. I didn't think of that."

He grinned. "The truck will be warm. Shall we go?"

She hesitated. "Let me stick these dishes in the dishwasher first."

He waited while she did so. She wanted to prolong their time together, but there wasn't much more to be done. "I should wipe the table."

"I'll get it." He grabbed a bottle of spray and a rag and headed out to the dining room. She stood in the doorway and watched. When he reached her he held out his hand. "Are we ready now?"

"I suppose." They went out the back door, and he locked up. She walked beside him back to his truck grateful for the time they'd had together. She wasn't sure if their attraction was mutual or if her feelings were unrequited. Was it possible she'd imagined his flirting? She didn't have enough experience with love to know. Did love explain the bittersweet ache taking over her emotions and controlling her life? If so, she wished she could turn it off, but then again, sometimes it felt pure and honest and she wanted it to last forever. To say she was confused would be putting it mildly. She was absolutely baffled by the emotions swimming inside her chest.

She forced her thoughts to quiet and concentrated on the sensation of his hand against her back. Did friends touch as often as they did? Daniel frequently reached for her hand, he put his arm around her, and sometimes his touch was more of a caress than a friendly gesture. Maybe their relationship was more than friendly, but if so, what did that make them? And why couldn't she scrounge up enough courage to come right out and ask him? She didn't want to date an unbeliever, but he wasn't one, right? He said he wasn't on speaking terms with

God. He didn't say he didn't believe. *Please, Lord, let him find his way back to you, not for my sake, but for his.*

~

IT'D BEEN a week since Dan took Ashley to Evelyn's. He continued to wrestle with himself over whether or not he should pursue a relationship with her. He'd told her that workplace romances were out of the question, and now he was breaking his own rule. The more often they spent time together the more it felt like a relationship despite her constant reminders that they were just friends. Taking her to his father's company Christmas party was definitely broadcasting to the world that she was his girlfriend whether they wanted to admit it or not.

Was he wrong to think she too desired more? He pulled up outside her house and hurried to her door.

She stood there with her evening bag in her left hand and her keys in her right.

"Looks like you're ready."

"I didn't want to make you late."

His gaze devoured her in the shimmery blue evening gown "You look amazing."

"Why thank you, kind sir." She batted her eyelashes.

He laughed. "Shall we go?"

She put on a long wool coat and they walked out to the truck together. He held out his hand to help her into the truck, and the scent of sweet peaches captivated him. "Aren't you the gentleman tonight?"

"The lady deserves special treatment."

ELLE E. KAY

She chuckled again.

On the drive to Denver, she broke the mood by detailing her nightmarish shopping experience trying to find an evening gown that fit her. He was glad she'd gone to so much effort since she looked magnificent, but he could've lived without the details of her excursion. The only thing he detested more than shopping was listening to people talk about shopping.

The huge room was decorated tastefully to resemble a winter wonderland. There were white snowflake decorations, silver balls, and shiny tinsel. Appetizing aromas drifted toward him, and he wondered how soon the food would be served. He was starved.

His father was ever the congenial host and welcomed Ashley with a hug and a kiss. He went to find his mother and keep her company while his father monopolized Ashley's attention. Once he'd located his mother, he brought her back to where Ashley and his father stood chatting and eating hor d'oeuvres. Hopefully, there wouldn't be any risk of shellfish exposure, but he'd made sure his mother brought an EpiPen just in case.

When Ashley finally broke free from his father, he took her around the room introducing her to his father's employees. Though he could tell she was wasn't comfortable in crowds, she handled the mingling with grace. He could sense her relief when they finally sat down to dinner, and the two of them could pay more attention to each other than the rest of the guests. When the meal was over, he held his hand out to her. "May I have this dance?"

"Certainly."

He led her to the dance floor where they were playing a song that would be good for a two-step. "Any chance you know how to two-step?"

She grinned. "It's my favorite dance next to the schottische."

"Well, I can't schottishe, but maybe you can teach me someday."

"I'd like that."

He spun her around the floor as a few other couples joined them.

~

ASHLEY SAVORED the feel of Dan's hand on her lower back. He spun her around three times, and when she came to a stop, she smiled up at him. His eyes crinkled at the corners, and she got lost in their deep green depths. Her carefully constructed wall fell at his feet. There was no protecting her heart now. It was his.

The song came to an end, and a waltz played. He pulled her closer.

"You're quite the dancer, Daniel."

"Only when I have a partner who knows how to follow a lead." He leaned in close, and whispered. "I think we make a good team for more than dancing."

"Is that so?" She searched his eyes to determine his meaning, but all she could see was amusement. Was he teasing her? She wondered if he knew she was in love with him, and was toying with her emotions. When the song ended, she pulled away. "I'm going to get some water."

"I'll get it for you."

She held out a hand. "No. I've got it. Thanks." She hurried

to a table that held bottled waters and grabbed one. After downing a few sips, she set it down and hurried to find a restroom. If she wasn't careful, she'd break down in front of Dan, and she didn't want him to know he had so much power over her emotions.

༶

TWO DAYS after the Christmas party, Dan opened the door to the kitchen.

Ashley smiled. "Hey."

"Come with me." He took her hand and pulled her outside, stopping for their coats on the way.

She took a moment to enjoy the view of the snow covered mountains surrounding them. "I'm supposed to be working. My boss shouldn't be the one preventing me from doing my job."

"You're taking a break." He pulled her around the back of the lodge where she noticed the daycare group out playing in the snow. "The daycare director sent an email asking for a volunteer to build a snowman and Sabrina volunteered me."

"What does that have to do with me?" Ashley asked.

"If I have to do this, I'm going to need a lovely assistant?"

"Why not Sabrina?"

His brow creased. "I didn't think of her. You're out here now. Are you going to help me or not?"

She positioned her hands like she was weighing a balance. "Go back to work or build a snowman with you?" She linked her arm with his, and grinned. "Easy choice."

They walked a few steps and then separated. Heat radiated through her chest, so to distract herself from what she was feeling she grabbed a handful of snow and tossed a snowball at him.

"Better watch it girl, or we'll be having a real snowball fight later."

"Threat or promise?"

He grabbed some snow and tucked it down the back of her coat. "Promise."

She tried to shake the snow out of her coat and keep up with his pace at the same time. Soon they were standing in front of fifteen children ranging in age from three to twelve and Dan demonstrated how to build a snowman. She made the head while he made the first two larger snow spheres.

They smoothed out the snow, and he added a scarf and a hat. The teacher handed him a carrot to use for the nose and a couple of stones for the eyes.

The children attempted to make their own snowmen, and they stayed to help. It was so much fun, she forgot to keep her guard up. When they headed back toward the kitchen, she was laughing and enjoying her time with Danny once again. The time she spent in his presence always ended with her losing another piece of herself.

She decided to bring up the faith issue. It might be a mistake to press him, but she couldn't let herself fall in love with him if he wasn't going to find his way back to church. "I'm leaving early to go to prayer meeting tonight."

"I'm aware."

"Any chance you'd want to join me?"

"No."

Her chest tightened. She shouldn't give him her heart, but it seemed it was too late.

10

Dan admired the Christmas lights as he drove home Thursday night. He hadn't had the time nor inclination to decorate himself but seeing the results of the town's efforts brought a smile to his face. Thinking back to the looks of joy on the kids' faces the previous day when he and Ashley had helped them build snowmen made him consider a future that included a good woman and children. It was insane for him to entertain such thoughts, and he knew it. Yet, when he'd walked through the kitchen earlier, the smile she sent his way pushed most of his doubts away.

He made the right-hand turn onto his road, and his stomach soured at what he saw there. Gage's truck was in his driveway. He parked beside it and got out. Gage opened his door and extended his hand in a wave. He didn't respond in kind.

He crossed his arms over his chest and stared down his former friend. "What are you doing here?"

"I think it's time we talked." Gage scratched at his neck.

As he stood there in a wide stance, he felt a vein pulsing at his throat. "I've got nothing to say."

ELLE E. KAY

"I do." Gage raked a hand through his hair.

"Then tell it to your shrink."

"Look, Dan, I know I screwed up with Ivy, and I'm sorry for that. I don't expect you to become my best bud again, but I see what you're doing to yourself and I can't stand by and stay quiet."

"What are you talking about?"

"God."

He let out a brittle laugh. "Leave it alone."

"No. I can't do that." He shook his head. "You preached to me when we were over there about a loving and forgiving God. Told me how pointless it was to beat myself up over things he'd already forgiven."

"Yeah. So?"

"Then I see you living in the past. What happened to being a new creature in Christ? Since you taught me about Christ's love and forgiveness, I started going to church. Even after all my mistakes and how I hurt you and Ivy, I'm living a new life. I've accepted God's forgiveness and have moved on, but I see the friend who led me to the Lord pulling away from Him. I get that you don't want to be around me, but I can find another church if that's what you want."

"I would never tell someone they couldn't go to my church."

"Except that is exactly what you've done… to yourself." Gage raked his fingers through his hair. "I won't stay and harp on it, but someone needed to say it, and I don't know many people with the guts to confront an Army Ranger, so I had to do it myself."

"I'm no longer active." He chuckled. "I'm a 68 Sierra."

"Didn't you get BRM in basic? What were they thinking letting a sharpshooter take a job in infection control?"

"I never was one for wearing diapers, so sniper was always out. That's why I went 89 Delta."

"Me too. Though, sometimes I wish I could turn back the clock and take a job that wouldn't have seen combat."

"I know what you mean."

"Look, Dan, I know we'll never be close like we were before. I betrayed your trust, and for what it's worth, I'm sorry. I'd give anything to take back that night. I get that you don't want to be friends, but can we try not to hate each other?"

He opened and closed his mouth before settling on an answer. "Sure. I'll see you around."

After Gage pulled out, he went inside and got himself a glass of cold water. First Ashley presses him on his faith and now Gage. Was it God trying to get his attention?

He didn't know what to make of Gage's visit. Was he concerned, or was it some kind of trick to get him to open up so he could use it against him? No. He knew Gage as well as he knew himself. That wasn't in his DNA. He'd messed up, but he hadn't set out with the intention of hurting anybody. He'd been trying to comfort Ivy and it led to more.

He shook his head. In the long run, he was better off. Now he was certain that Ivy wasn't the woman for him, and if that indiscretion had never happened, he would've married the wrong woman. If he wanted Ashley though, he had to accept all that came with dating her. She would expect his faith to be as strong as hers.

Could he get that back? Was it possible to renew his relationship with Almighty God?

∽

THE NIGHT was crisp and cold. Wind bit into his cheeks as he watched the parade. Light poles along the route were lined with giant snowflakes. It was a sight to behold and Dan hoped Ashley would appreciate it as much as he did. The Freedom High School Marching band started the parade off, followed by a float designed to look like the scenery from the nutcracker. The tiny ballerinas from the local dance school manned the float looking adorable in their costumes though he hoped they had their coats tucked away somewhere since the night grew colder by the minute.

Ashley smiled and pointed to the firetruck with the characters on board tossing candy to the children.

He grinned. "Did you want some candy, darling?"

She laughed. "I was pointing out the dogs coming up behind the firetruck?"

"So, you're an animal fan?" He glanced across the street and saw a couple kissing. What would Ashley do if he pulled her to him and kissed her like that? Would she respond or would she push him away? He reached for her hand and laced his fingers with her gloved ones.

"Who doesn't love animals?" Her head tilted to the side.

"Did I tell you I adopted a dog?"

"You haven't mentioned it, no. When did you do that?"

"About a month ago when you were mad at me. I needed a friend to hang out with, so I adopted Sammy."

"I don't remember being mad at you."

"Trust me. You were."

"What kind of dog did you get?"

"A husky mix."

"Can I meet him?" Ashely's face tilted toward his.

"Sure. How about tonight?" His gaze dropped to her lips. The urge to kiss her intensified. His hand went to the back of her head and his thumb caressed her jawline. He looked in her eyes, they clouded over, and she took a step back.

"What's wrong?"

"There's something I need to tell you. Something I should've told you weeks ago."

"What?"

"I overheard a conversation Ivy had with a man and they were plotting something against someone."

"What are you talking about?"

"There was mention of payments and a truck being moved. The more I considered it, the more I believed it was you they were targeting, but I'm still not certain. I think the guy was paying Ivy to mess with you. When Ivy walked past us a few minutes ago, she was with a guy. He spoke, and if I'm not mistaken, it was the same man I heard at the lodge. He's here with her now. They disappeared into the Freedom Fudge Factory a moment ago."

He flinched. "And you didn't tell me? I thought we were friends?"

"I was afraid you wouldn't believe me over Ivy, and I

wasn't positive they were talking about you. Before I decided what to do a considerable amount of time had passed, so I knew you'd be angry that I hadn't yet told you."

He let out a bitter laugh. "Angry doesn't begin to cover it." He sucked in a breath ignoring the bite from the cold air entering his lungs. He closed his eyes, and his hand absently rubbed his chest. When he opened his eyes, Ashley remained rooted to the ground in front of him. The crowd had begun to disperse, and the couple he'd seen kissing disappeared from sight. "If you didn't trust me enough to come to me, you could've gone to Kevin or Heath. Even Mr. Harrington would've listened."

She reached for his arm, but he evaded her touch. "But, Daniel I did go to—"

"I'll drive you home." He took a step back and let out a forceful breath.

A tear slid down her cheek, but he stalked ahead leaving her to trail behind. He didn't care that she'd need to run to keep pace with him. She'd brought it on herself.

How could he have been so stupid? Nothing favorable had ever come from trusting a woman in the past. Why had he expected Ashley to be different?

~

ASHLEY OPENED the passenger door of Dan's truck and hoisted herself up onto the seat. She swiped at her tears with gloved fingers. Tears wouldn't help matters. She snuck a glance over at Dan. His hands were clenched on the steering wheel and his lips were pinched tight, but he hadn't started the vehicle. He had a legitimate reason to be angry. She'd brought this on herself. She'd had weeks to come clean about the conversation she'd heard, but instead of telling him, she'd kept it to herself.

"What did he look like?" He started the truck and pulled out into the heavy traffic leaving the parade.

"Who?"

"Don't play dumb, Ashley. The man who paid Ivy. What did he look like? I can't go after him while you're with me, but I'd like to know who he is, so I can deal with him later."

"I couldn't see him when I overheard them talking."

"But you think he was with her tonight? Did you see him clearly?"

"Tall, blond hair. I didn't notice eye color."

He pinched the bridge of his nose. "You're saying he looks like me?"

"Less girth, but honestly, he could pass for your brother."

"Any distinguishing characteristics?"

"No."

"Great. I can't think of any tall thin blond men who are out to harm me, and I didn't notice Ivy tonight. I was too wrapped-up in you."

The words were bittersweet to her ears. He'd enjoyed her company enough that he hadn't paid attention to Ivy, but she'd gone and messed things up beyond repair. She needed to stay focused on the conversation and not daydream about what could've been if she'd told him sooner. "The man wasn't necessarily thin, just not as wide in the shoulders as you."

He sighed. "I'll have to ask Ivy."

"I'm sorry, Dan. I truly am."

A vein bulged in his neck. "Your crocodile tears and apologies are meaningless. You should think about looking for a job. I'm not sure I can continue to work with you."

"You're firing me?"

"No. I'm not firing you. I'm asking you to consider leaving of your own accord." He raked his fingers through his hair. "I thought— Nevermind. It doesn't matter what I thought. I was wrong, but if you have an ounce of decency in you, go home to Pennsylvania and leave me in peace." He pulled into her driveway before turning his cold stare on her.

She slumped in her seat, letting her tears fall freely. He had no idea what it would cost her to leave, but if that was what he desired, she'd do it. The last thing she wanted to do was hurt him more than she already had. "Okay. I'll go."

He nodded and waited for her to get out of the truck. She jogged to her front door and let herself in. Even in his anger, Dan waited until she was safely inside before driving away. It was something. He must still care for her a little.

11

Dan slammed his foot on the brake at the sound of mortar fire. His truck spun out of control on the snow-covered road before coming to a stop.

Missiles exploded in every direction. The pungent odor of burning flesh and gun powder turned his stomach.

He struggled to exit his vehicle and scanned the horizon for the enemy.

All he could see were colorful lights illuminating the night sky.

He sunk to his knees. Fireworks. It was fireworks. He'd almost lost touch with reality and retreated into the recesses of his mind where war still raged. Would he ever stop reliving it?

Lord, help.

The prayer drifted up before he could stop it.

He'd trusted the Lord to help, but God hadn't prevented the bomb his men had been diffusing from exploding. His friends had died, and he'd been allowed to live.

Why?

It was the one question he couldn't stop asking the Almighty even after he'd turned away from Him.

He climbed back into his truck and snatched up the photograph of his buddies that sat in his console. The men he should've protected with his own life were dead. Their families mourned them while he got to come home to his own family and to Ivy.

Ivy. He turned the key in the ignition and turned the truck back toward town. He needed answers and they wouldn't wait until morning.

As he pounded on her door, he felt his pulse increase. She didn't answer.

Before he made it back to his truck, her Mustang pulled into the driveway, and she turned off the ignition, slid out of the sports car, and grinned. "Hello, sexy. Decide to take me up on my offer?"

"What offer would that be?" He walked up to her car.

"To get back together." The corner of her mouth lifted in a smile.

He put his hands on the car, one on each side of her effectively pinning her in place. Her smile widened, and she looped her arms around his neck. He leaned in close and whispered in her ear. "Ain't never gonna happen, babe."

She brought a knee up, but he sidestepped it. "What are you doing here, Danny?" The syrupy sweet tone was gone from her voice.

"I want to know whose paying you to torment me."

"I'm sure I don't know what you're talking about."

"Don't play games, Ivy. I know about the scheme."

"His name is Sean. I don't know his last name."

"Don't lie to me!" He pounded a fist on her car hood.

Taking a step back, she crossed her arms over her chest. "You're scaring me."

"Good!"

She unlocked her front door and let herself in, leaving the door open for him to enter. "Have a seat. Do you want something to drink?"

"This isn't a social visit." He scowled.

She sat down and lowered her elbows to her knees resting her head in her hands. "I don't know what I've gotten myself into. The guy was cute and friendly, so when he first approached me about playing some pranks on you, I thought it would be fun. I thought it might bring you and I back together and give us something to laugh about later." She reached her hand out to him, but he shook his head. "But then he got scary."

Dan flexed his fingers. Just what he needed was a sob story from his ex-fiancée. "How so?"

"He ordered me to up my game. He told me to put the fear of God in you."

"The fear of God never left me. He needn't have worried about that." His laughter had a hard edge to it.

"I was supposed to cut your brake lines."

"You're serious?" He grimaced.

She wiped away a tear. "I didn't do it."

"Did you consider it?" He rubbed the back of his neck.

Looking down at her hands, she said, "Sean scares me."

He shook his head. "You did. You gave it serious thought. Are you aware you could've spent the rest of your life in prison if you'd have cut my brake lines, and I was killed in an automobile accident?"

She nodded.

"Where did you meet this Sean guy?"

"At the Liberty Grille. I waited on him."

"And when did the conversation about me come up?"

"He asked me out. We went out one night and I must've mentioned you. He claimed you two were friends overseas, and he wished to play a practical joke on you. I agreed. It sounded fun."

"What happened next?"

"He never called again, but then one day he cornered me at work and got all weird at that point."

"So, you're responsible for the crazy stuff happening of late?"

She stood and smoothed her skirt down with her hands. "I'm sorry, Danny. I didn't know how to get out of it once I was in."

"You could've come to me."

"And told you that I'd made a deal with some nutcase to harass you?" Her chin quivered.

"It would've been an apt place to start."

Her eyes grew glassy, and she tucked her chin to her chest.

"Tell me, Ivy, exactly how much was my peace of mind worth? Five hundred, one thousand?" His nostrils flared, and he stood.

Her shoulders drooped, but she didn't answer the question. "I said I was sorry."

He started toward the door before turning back to face her again. "How did you get a key?"

"I had it made when we were together."

"Why?"

"When you were first deployed, I slept in your bed most nights. Being surrounded by your things and having the scent of your cologne on the sheets gave me a sense of comfort."

"You didn't need me. You had no trouble finding comfort in my best friend's arms."

"That's not fair."

"Isn't it?"

"You signed up to play with bombs! How did you think that made me feel? Do you have any idea what it was like waiting for a phone call telling me you'd blown yourself up trying to diffuse a roadside bomb? When Gage came home injured and told me what happened, I was distraught, he was sympathetic and comforting, and, well, one thing led to another. I didn't mean for it to happen."

"But it did."

"Yes, it did. You have no idea how badly I want to turn back the clock and have a redo on that evening."

"That's not how it works, babe." He moved to the door and let himself out, pulling the door shut behind him. The cold air stung his sweat drenched skin. A deep breath of icy air burned his lungs, and he looked up at the night sky. Sporadic fireworks continued to light the atmosphere. He wished the locals would get a clue as to the true cost of those elaborate displays. If he were a nice guy, he'd go visit Gage and make sure he wasn't reliving their mutual nightmare, but he couldn't forgive and forget. Not yet. He could, however, ask Van to check on Gage. He sent a quick text and got into his truck to head home.

ASHLEY TOSSED and turned but couldn't get the look in Daniel's eyes out of her mind. She'd hurt him. All this time, she'd been worried about how easily he could break her heart, but she hadn't for a moment considered that she'd have the power to cause him pain. Yet, she had.

Such a simple thing. An overheard conversation that she shouldn't have eavesdropped on to begin with. Why hadn't she told him when it happened? She'd been almost certain they'd been talking about him, but there was that tiny chance she was wrong, and she didn't want to falsely accuse Ivy, but more than that she was worried that Ivy would deny it and he'd believe his ex-fiancée over his chef.

She hadn't considered that he might trust her despite his lack of interest in her romantically. She'd been a fool.

She gave up on sleep and got out of bed. Maybe a bowl of ice cream would help her cope, but no. There was nothing to be done about her heartache. She'd brought it on herself, so she needed to face it. First thing in the morning, she would put in her notice and make travel arrangements for her trip home after the New Year.

It would be pleasant to see her family even though the circumstances could've been better. Going home a failure hadn't been part of the plan, and she could already hear the disappointment in her father's voice, but it couldn't be helped.

～

SEAN WAITED outside Winchester's girlfriend's house. He'd seen them together at the parade and had watched from inside the store as Army boy stalked away from his girl. Winchester might be able to fool himself, but there was no doubt in Sean's mind that if he wanted to hurt him, the way to do it was to go through Ashley Castle.

Winchester's feelings for the woman were unmistakable. Forget Ivy's little mind games. The way to get to the staff sergeant was through the woman he loved, and it was now clear that Ivy wasn't that woman.

The longer he watched him with the chef, the more convinced he was. Ms. Castle would need to die for the greater good.

He pulled back onto the road. His date wouldn't wait forever. It was the third time he'd arrived late since they'd started seeing each other, but she let him get away with it. His attractiveness and charm made it easy for women to overlook his shortcomings.

When he arrived at the lodge, he parked and walked into the lobby. He found his girl waiting in the lounge area with two cups of coffee from the Mountain Mug in her hands.

"You're late." She handed him one of the coffees.

"Pumpkin Latte with extra sugar?"

"Yep."

"Thanks, sweetie." He kissed her cheek.

12

Dan arrived at the office early hoping to avoid Ashley altogether. If he stayed in his office and used the hall entrance to reach the dining room instead of going through the kitchen, he might not run into her. A restaurant manager shouldn't be avoiding the kitchen, but soon she would be gone, and everything would go back to normal. If there was such a thing as normal.

Her stormy eyes came to mind, and he remembered how they shone with tears as she climbed into his truck the previous night. She'd broken down his barriers and gotten close. He'd nearly kissed her. If the night had gone as planned, they would've left the parade a couple, but he wouldn't hand her the knife so she could stab him in the back. Secrets had a way of spiraling out of control.

If he'd known about the discussion she'd overheard, he would've realized it wasn't a housekeeper his mother hired that was making changes around his home. It would've occurred to him to install security cameras and ask Heath in the security office to keep watch for the man that Ashley had heard talking to Ivy.

A soft knock on his office door put a stop to his train of

thought. "Come in."

"Can we talk?" Ashley's eyes glistened, and a stab of guilt shot through his gut.

He didn't have anything to feel guilty about. He wasn't the one concealing matters. He'd been prepared to take a chance with her and give her his heart. His posture stiffened. "What do you want, Ms. Castle?"

"It's like that, then?"

"Yes, ma'am."

"Fine. I came to let you know that I put in my two-week's notice as you requested. I'll be heading home soon."

"Good." He stood. "Is that all?"

"That's it."

"I have a question for you?"

"What's that?"

"Do you know what day it was that you overheard Ivy's conversation?"

"I don't recall, but I do know that it was the day that Thomas started."

"Thank you. I'll see if security can pull up footage, so I can learn who the man was."

"Can't you ask Ivy?"

"I did. She doesn't know his last name."

"That's weird."

"I thought so, too. Send Carly in when she arrives."

"Will do."

When Ashley closed the door behind her, he let out a breath he hadn't realized he was holding. He picked up his phone and dialed the extension for Jeff Wallace.

"HR. Jeff Wallace speaking."

"It's Dan, Jeff. Would you mind checking to see what date it was that Thomas started in the kitchen?"

"Is there a problem with the kid?"

"No. No problem. In fact, he might be promoted earlier than expected, but I need you to check on the date for another reason."

"Sure thing. I'll get back to you in a few minutes."

When the telephone rang a few minutes later, he had his answer.

～

DAN TURNED his office chair around and looked out over the peaks and valleys of the mountain range. His heart felt like it'd been torn from his chest. He shouldn't have let Ashley get close. He knew women couldn't be trusted, but he'd been ready to take a leap of faith and try again with her. He'd believed in his heart that she was the real deal. That maybe she was the one woman he could trust. What a fool he'd been.

The buzz of his intercom interrupted his musing, so he flipped his chair around and answered it.

"I have Max on the line."

"Thanks, Sabrina. Put him through."

"Hey Max. What's up?"

"The results are finally in from the plates, cups, and utensils we tested after your father's party. The lab wouldn't prioritize the testing since we assumed the poisoning was accidental," Max said.

"What are you talking about?"

"Heath and Ashley didn't mention that we were testing everything from the banquet?"

"No. Neither one of them said a word."

"We tested everything. The only trace we found was on your father's water glass. The weird thing is it was from a type of crab that isn't served at Liberty Grille. Our conclusion is that your father was intentionally poisoned. Someone knew he had an allergy and used that information to send him to the hospital. If you hadn't been there to call for help, he may not have survived."

"Wow. You're telling me someone tried to kill my father?" He rubbed the back of his neck.

"That's what I'm saying, yes."

"Do you have any suspects?" Dan asked

"That's the other thing I wanted to talk to you about." There was a long pause. "Ivy's fingerprints were on the glass."

"She works at Liberty Grille."

"Yes, but she wasn't working the banquet."

"She wasn't supposed to be, but she was in there talking to my parents."

"Do you think she laced your father's glass?" Max asked

"Just yesterday, I would've said no."

"What happened yesterday?"

"Ivy admitted that she'd considered cutting my brake lines."

"I'm going to have to bring her in for questioning."

"Do you have any other enemies? Ashley said something about a conversation Ivy had with some other guy."

"When did she tell you about that?"

"As soon as you left for the hospital the day of the party."

"At least she bothered telling someone," Dan said.

"She didn't tell you?"

"Not until last night."

"You're ticked?"

"You know it."

"Back to the enemies. Do you have any?" Max asked.

"Gage isn't my biggest fan."

"I don't think we have reason to suspect Gage, but we're going to have to take a serious look at Ivy since she was working the day of the incident and her fingerprints were on the glass"

"I still think it's a stretch that Ivy would try to kill my dad, Max," Dan said.

"I hope you're right."

"I should probably mention the other weird stuff."

"What kind of weird stuff?"

"Promise not to call me crazy?"

"Nope. If the straight-jacket fits..."

"Fine. Well, first someone turned off my hall light and washed my sheets."

"Straight-jacket is looking like it might fit."

"After that, someone moved my truck into the garage."

"So, you think these events are related?"

"Don't you?"

"I don't put much stock in coincidence. So, it's likely related."

"Ivy admitted to being responsible for some of what happened, but she claimed she was being coerced."

"By whom?"

"She only had a first name. Sean."

"Convenient." Max cleared his throat. "Do you know anybody named Sean who might hold a grudge against you or your father?"

"I don't."

"Have you kept a log of the so-called weird stuff?"

"No. I didn't write anything down, but if I go back through my calendar, I can figure out a dozen or so things that seemed odd or out of place."

"Do that. Get me that list ASAP."

"Yes, sir."

"And Danny?"

"Yeah?"

"Watch your back." Max sighed. "You could be in serious

HEALING THE HERO

trouble."

"I will. Thanks." Dan sat there after he hung up the phone contemplating Max's call. He'd believed that Ashley didn't care, but maybe she did. She'd cared enough to go to the police. Why had she thought he'd believe Ivy over her? What had he done to give her that impression?

∽

DAN'S OFFICE was in the corner of the lodge behind the Liberty Grille, and the security office was tucked into the opposite corner all the way on the other side of the lodge out of sight of guests. He headed in that direction but stopped at the Mountain Mug on his way through the resort.

Casey set a black coffee on the counter for him, and he tossed down some cash and grabbed it. He didn't even have enough energy to muster up a smile for the barista. Hopefully, she'd understand. Everyone had their off days.

The door to the security office was ajar, but Heath was intently staring at the monitors, so he knocked to alert the big man that he was there.

"It's been a while, Dan. What brings you by?"

"I need a favor."

"Sure thing." Heath grinned. "What can I do for you?"

"On November 15th, we had a new hire start. On that same day, Ms. Castle overheard a conversation between one of our waitresses and a man she couldn't identify, I'm wondering if you can find footage so I can see if I recognize the guy."

"She mentioned something about that after your dad's party." Heath raised an eyebrow. "What's with the Ms. Castle? I thought you and Ashley were friends."

"We were."

"I think I must be missing something, and I'm guessing it has to do with this footage you want to see."

"You're an astute man."

"Where do you want me to focus?"

"The camera on the exit door near my office."

The security guard pulled up the footage and slowed it down when he saw Dan's office door opening. "It's not the best angle, but we should be able to see anyone who comes down the hall and goes into any of the rooms near that end of the hall or out the back door."

"Stop it there." He looked closer. "Is Ashley crying?"

"Looks like it." Heath glanced up at Dan. "Let's not invade her privacy though, I'm going to fast-forward past her."

The next person the image showed was Ivy coming out of the locker room followed a few minutes later by a man he couldn't identify, but who looked vaguely familiar. The man left through the back-exit door. "Would you get me a still picture of that guy, please?"

"Sure thing." After hitting a few buttons, Heath sent the image to the printer, and Dan picked it up from there.

"Thanks for this."

"It's my job."

"Above and beyond the call of duty, friend."

The big man grinned. "Make sure you update Kevin and Mr. Harrington on what's going on."

"I will." Dan hurried back to his office hoping to sort out why a man he didn't know would want to kill him. Ivy had said he'd wanted her to cut his brake lines, and on snowy mountain roads that would mean near certain death.

TWO HOURS later, Dan sat hunched over his desk. Something about the video was eating at him. He wondered why Ashley had been crying when she left his office. Had he caused that? Thinking back on the day in question, he remembered he'd been running late. It was the day when he'd thought Ashley was flirting with Thomas. He'd overreacted, and if the video showed what he thought it did, he'd made her cry.

He stared at the photograph he'd had Heath print and contemplated whether he should ask his friend in the FBI to run it through facial recognition and see if there were any hits. It seemed like an extreme measure for harassment complaints, but after his conversation with Ivy and Max's call, he wasn't so sure that was all this was.

If he told Kevin, he knew Kevin would update Mr. Harrington. He was going to have to tell both of them before Max did. He reached for the phone, but a knock on his door made him drop his hand.

His door opened a crack. "Hey, Danny-boy. You wanted to see me?"

"Come in." He stood and pointed to a chair across from his desk. "Have a seat."

"What's up?"

"Did Ms. Castle tell you she put in her notice?"

"What!? No way. Ashley loves her job here."

"I asked her to resign, Carly."

"You did what!?" Carly jumped to her feet. "What is wrong with you? A decent woman comes into your life, and what do you do? You push her away? Is that it?"

He felt his face burn as his temper rose, and he stood. "You're out of line."

"Maybe you should ask me to quit, too. Would that work for you?"

"Stop it."

"I will not stop, Danny. Ashley is my friend, and she's madly in love with you, but you're too wrapped up in self-loathing to even notice her. What did she do, Dan? Smile at you the wrong way?"

"That's not fair, and you know it."

"Isn't it?"

He slammed both hands down on his desk even though he wanted to wrap them around his friend's throat. "She lied by omission. She knew something important and kept it from me for weeks."

"And you think that means she should have to lose her job and uproot her life? You know there are no other jobs like hers in Freedom. She'll have to start over someplace else."

"I'm aware."

"Than you're a selfish ogre."

"Take the rest of the day off, Carly. You're dismissed."

ASHLEY ARRIVED home later than usual. Dan had sent Carly home, so she'd had to handle the busy Saturday crowd without her sous chef. Her dessert chef was upset that a special chocolate he ordered hadn't arrived. Her junior chef didn't appreciate having to take on half of Carly's duties, and the rest of the kitchen staff were tense and uneasy throughout the night.

They most likely knew that she'd given her notice and realized it would mean big changes for them. Though she sympathized, there wasn't a thing she could do about it. If she hadn't resigned, she'd have been fired. Dan had all but said as much.

It was her own fault. How many times had she mulled over that conversation in her mind and practiced telling him about it? If she'd followed through sooner, maybe the confrontation at the parade wouldn't have happened. Maybe they'd still be friends.

Would being Dan's friend be any better than being banished from his life? If the pain she'd experienced in the weeks leading up to their fight were any indication, she might be better off back home. It was excruciating spending so much time with someone who'd become a close friend when she longed for so much more from him. It wasn't fair to him either. He needed a friend, and she couldn't be that friend when she couldn't stop thinking about what it would be like for him to kiss her.

She shook her head. The day had been grueling, and she needed to get some rest before tomorrow arrived. If she knew Carly as well as she thought she did, the girl wouldn't show up at work tomorrow. She'd be stewing over her conversation with Dan. Which meant that even though it was supposed to be her day off, she would be stuck at work for another exhausting day. It was time for some shuteye.

Three hours later, she looked at her clock. Sleep was elusive, and it didn't care about work.

The resort was packed with people who'd come to celebrate Christmas in the Rockies. She'd been looking forward to it herself, but as the day drew near, it'd lost its appeal. What she wanted now was to go home and see her mom and dad. She yearned for the company of family, and longed to see her siblings. Christmas with family would be far preferable to spending it at the lodge, but her two weeks brought her all the way to New Year's Day.

She wondered if Dan would miss her. A bitter laugh escaped. Of course he wouldn't. What had she thought would happen? It was her own doing, so now she had to face the consequences of her decisions.

13

Dan walked into the kitchen grateful Ashley wouldn't be there with her sad eyes. Two steps into the kitchen he caught of whiff of her peach shampoo and realized his mistake. She stood at the sink filling a pot with water.

"What are you doing here?" His tone was sharp.

"What does it look like I'm doing, Dan?"

"Where's Carly?" He straightened his posture until he stood rigidly awaiting her answer.

Her chin lifted slightly. "She's still not speaking to you, apparently. I received a text this morning when I got home from the early service. She isn't coming in."

He made eye contact with Ashley. "Do you blame me, too?"

She set down the pot a little too forcefully. "No. I blame myself."

His feet felt like they were glued to the floor. How was he supposed to respond to that?

"Look, Danny. I'm here until January 1st. I don't want us to have to avoid each other until then. We both know what happened was entirely my fault, but don't take it out on the rest of the staff. Let's at least be cordial to each other while we're here."

He nodded. "Do you think Carly will come around soon or do I need to find a new chef?"

"Carly is not a head chef. You should start the search for a new chef whether she stays or goes. It will take another three or four years before she is ready to handle the pressures of a kitchen this size. She could easily handle a smaller place on her own, but she isn't ready for this."

"You don't think she'll rise to the challenge?"

"Carly is a firecracker, and she'll give it her all, but if you throw her into this unprepared, you'll be responsible for her failure. I honestly don't believe you want that."

"No. Of course not."

"Besides, if she takes a day off when she's upset with her boss, she might not have the maturity for the job."

He scratched the stubble on his chin. "True."

"I heard someone mention Jacques was back in town."

"I'd rather quit myself than hire him back."

"You're going to need to hire someone."

"Will you stay until I find the right person?"

Her shoulders drooped. "I don't think that's a good idea. I'm not handling the deterioration of our friendship well. If I stay, it'll only be harder on both of us."

It was true. As much as he didn't want to have to rush to find a replacement for Ashley, if she stayed any longer than necessary, he'd be tempted to forgive her, and if he did that, he'd be opening himself up to more pain. "I understand."

"Van can run the kitchen until you find someone. It will hurt Carly's feelings, but if you want to keep things running smoothly, he's your guy. I don't think he'd be interested in the position permanently, but it wouldn't hurt to ask."

"I never even considered him."

"I suggest you do."

He went back to his office and sank into his chair. His conversation with Ashley went well. Though he could see her pain, she didn't lash out at him or try to make him feel guilty. Not that he needed any encouragement in that department. He rubbed at his chest absently.

Ashley had once again proven helpful. Van was their dessert chef, but she was correct that he was more than capable of handling the pressures of running the kitchen. He'd proven that with his time in the service. He worked well with Van, and promoting him wouldn't cause too much disruption in the kitchen.

<hr />

A SOUND downstairs caught Ashley's attention. The house made noise sometimes, so she listened to see if she would hear it again and she did, but it didn't sound like anything she'd heard before. There was a strange splashing sound followed by some clunking noises. She rose to her feet and slipped on a pair of pajama pants.

Her father had taught her to shoot, but she hadn't brought a handgun with her. She hadn't been sure about the laws in Colorado, and she hadn't had time to look into them. Going down the stairs slowly so as to not make any noise, she spotted a man in her kitchen.

She ducked down out of sight, but it was too late. He'd seen her.

"Aren't you a cute little thing?" The man drew out his words. "This is the first time I've seen you up close that you weren't bundled up in a coat. It's too bad you have such poor taste in men."

"Who are you?"

He smirked, and recognition dawned. "The man who is going to make Daniel Winchester pay for his sins." The tall blond man would've been attractive if he wasn't standing in her house with a gas can in his hand.

She kicked the man in his knee and ran to the door.

He grabbed her arm and yanked her back. "If I hadn't poured the gas, I would take my time with you. You might want to count your blessings that you'll likely pass out from smoke inhalation before the fire gets you. It's too bad about the gasoline. I would've enjoyed some quality time alone with you."

Bile rose in her throat, and she clawed at the man's face.

"Just for that, I won't knock you out. You can experience the fire firsthand."

A scream tore from her throat.

He grabbed her wrist and pulled her into the kitchen.

She kicked him.

He slapped her, and she tasted blood.

She fought back, but he was strong.

He pushed her ahead of him into the garage. A roll of duct tape sat on her workbench. He grabbed it and wound it around her wrists.

Once she was secured, he pulled her by her hair to the far corner of the garage. Tears sprang to her eyes.

He pulled down the ladder that led to the storage loft. "This will do fine." He tossed her on his shoulder and took the first step.

She shifted her weight causing him to stumble back down the steps.

He let out a string of profanity. His fists pummeled her. He grabbed the duct tape and used his teeth to tear a piece off. "This'll work. You're duct tape came in handy." He used it to attach her to the built-in ladder leading upstairs. "It won't take long."

Please, Lord, help me.

The man took her garage door opener out of her car. He let himself out.

She screamed. A neighbor might hear and call 911. Her hopes were dashed when he tossed a match and walked away.

The fire spread. It was so hot.

Tears streaked down her face burning the open wounds.

She curled up in a ball and tried to breathe through her shirt. It was hopeless. If she'd known today would be her last, she would've tried harder to fix things with Daniel. She sat up and picked at the duct tape. It took too long. She fought for breath.

The tape tore, and she ran.

ELLE E. KAY

As she passed her car the dizziness claimed her. She collapsed.

Lord, help. Please.

Her world went dark.

~

DAN DROVE down Ashley's street. He couldn't say why. It was his habit to use the next street over to reach his house. His truck seemed to go down Ashley's road of its own accord.

He saw her front door was wide open as he passed by. She wouldn't leave her door open in the dead of night. And not when it was ten degrees.

A deep breath calmed him. He backed up and pulled in her drive.

He didn't want to fight. But he couldn't forget what she'd done.

He put the truck in park and got out. When he reached the door, he saw her cat walking on the porch rail. "Where's your owner, Ginger?"

Leaning in the front door, he hollered, "Ashley!"

No response came.

He went in and called to the cat, but she wouldn't budge from her spot on the porch. He pulled the door shut with a last glance back at the cat.

He moved to the stairs and yelled, "Ashley! Where are you?"

She didn't answer. Her car wasn't in the drive.

Maybe she'd gone out and left it open. There was only one way to know for sure. He'd check the garage for her car.

He pushed open the man door that led into her garage. A wave of heat and smoke knocked him down.

Flames engulfed her car and half the garage.

He didn't see her.

He pulled his t-shirt up over his mouth and nose. He tried to avoid the flames as he crawled into the garage. The smoke was thick. He coughed through the thin fabric of his shirt.

He saw her through the smoke and moved to her.

She lay face down on the floor. There wasn't much time before he suffered the same fate.

His t-shirt fell from his face. He scooped her into his arms.

Swatting at the flames that engulfed her clothes, he ran.

The open door was barely visible through the smoke. He moved toward it.

Uncontrollable coughing overtook him as he carried her toward the kitchen. He dropped her and collapsed on the floor. He checked her pulse.

She was alive, but unconscious.

He had to get her out before the fire spread through the rest of the house.

He dug out his phone and dialed 911. The smoke prevented him from speaking clearly. He hoped the dispatcher would send help.

He scooped Ashley back into his arms, stumbling as he did and moved further through her kitchen.

ELLE E. KAY

An explosion rocked the house. They were thrown apart by the force of the blast.

He struggled to his knees, and searched for her. He spotted her on her back with her neck bent at an odd angle. He crawled to her praying she was alive, and that he'd reach her before it was too late.

~

THE SOUND of sirens pierced the night and Dan knew in that moment that God sent them.

Someone else might've called 911 before he had, but the distance of the fire station to Ashley's house was too great for them to have arrived on scene that quickly. He hadn't seen any smoke when he'd arrived and though it felt longer, he knew it had only been a few minutes. The thickness of the smoke made praying aloud impossible, but silent prayers of gratitude proceeded from his soul and spirit. He knew in that moment that he'd been blaming God for the actions of man, and that if he wanted to renew the peace he'd once known, he needed to restore his relationship with Jesus.

There was a loud bang as a fireman kicked in the door. The next thing he knew there were hands on him attempting to drag him from the burning building. He was coughing too hard to speak, so he pulled himself free and pushed the firefighter toward Ashley.

The man lifted her easily and hurried outside as the blaze closed in.

Dan followed them to where the EMTs waited across the street. The fresh air started another coughing fit and he bent over at the waist until he could breathe again. An EMT rushed to help him to the van. He recognized him as Carson, the man who helped with his father. Once there, he was helped onto a stretcher and a mask was fitted to his face. Soon the oxygen they gave him eased the spasms in his lungs, and he was able to breathe albeit painfully. He pulled the mask from his face. "The cat. Someone has to get her cat. Last I saw Ginger she was on the porch rail."

"We'll look for her."

A few minutes later a female firefighter joined them, and she had Ginger curled up in her arms. "We'll keep your friend's cat safe until she can be reunited with her."

He nodded his thanks.

DAN WAS transported to Martin County Veterans' Memorial Hospital by ambulance and allowed the medical professionals to look him over though he wanted nothing more than to be at Ashley's side.

The doctor came into his room and picked up a clipboard. She didn't even glance up at him as she read his chart.

"Excuse me."

The doctor raised her eyes to meet his.

"I need to get out of here. My friend was brought in with me, and I want to be by her side."

"Let me look you over. Your vitals were normal when the nurse checked them, so if everything checks out, I'll have them prepare your discharge paperwork."

"Thanks."

After a cursory examination, the doctor left the room, and

he was left alone until the nurse brought the discharge paperwork more than forty-five minutes later. He hurried to the desk to find out where Ashley was. Max was there. "Hey Max. Do you know where they brought her?"

"Yeah. She was moved to a regular room. They want to keep her overnight."

"Can I see her?"

"Of course. Let me go get her room number."

He hurried off and came back with the room number a minute later. "Didn't want to ask the desk clerk?"

"With that scowl on her face, I was afraid she might throw something at me."

Dan held up a piece of paper with the room number on it. "Ask and ye shall receive." He smiled. "She was perfectly pleasant."

"Hmm." Max's ears turned a little red as he glanced at the girl behind the desk. "Who'd have thunk it?"

"I'm going to head over to Ashley's room."

"Call me if she wakes up," Max said.

"Will do."

When he reached Ashley's room, he peered in to make sure she was alone, and walked slowly to her bedside, afraid he might disturb her. He gently lifted her hand from where it lay on top of the blankets and kissed it. There were marks around her wrists from where she'd been duct taped. What kind of monster binds a woman and leaves her in a burning building?

If he got his hands on the perpetrator, the man wouldn't

live to tell about it. A still small voice nudged at him from somewhere within. A voice long ago buried reminded him that revenge was not the answer, and a verse came to mind.

> *Dearly beloved, avenge not yourselves, but rather give place unto wrath: for it is written, Vengeance is mine; I will repay, saith the Lord.*

He recognized it as a New Testament Bible verse that referred to an old-testament verse, but his memory verses were fuzzy and he couldn't recall book, chapter, and verse number or what his mentor referred to as the address of the scripture.

He studied Ashley's delicate features marred by the beating she'd received before he'd arrived. If they hadn't been at odds would she have stayed late to help him close up? Was what happened to her his fault? He sank into the chair by her bed and prayed. He poured out his heart asking forgiveness for blaming God for what happened in Afghanistan.

He felt God's peace surround him as if God was telling him to stop assigning guilt and blame. It wasn't his fault. He couldn't have known that someone was watching with a remote detonator. There was no way for him to know that as soon as his men were in place the device would explode. Maybe he should've known. They could've done more recon, but hindsight was always clearer, and he'd done the best he could with the information he'd had.

Night turned to dawn as he prayed and held Ashley's delicate hand in his. He didn't want to lose her. He'd asked her to resign, but the more he thought about it, the more he realized he'd been unreasonable. Yes, she should've told him what she'd heard, but she couldn't have known what he'd been going through.

He hadn't shared his fears that he was going insane with her. Hadn't told her that someone was messing with him. If she didn't know, how could she be expected to know the importance of what she'd overheard? He sighed.

He lifted his head when he heard a light rapping on the open door. Carly stood there. There were tears streaming down her face. He got to his feet and pulled her to him. They embraced for a full minute.

"She's out of the woods, isn't she?" Carly asked.

"We'll know more when she wakes up, but the doctors think her injuries are superficial. They remain concerned about her lungs though."

"That's a relief."

"Can you stay with her for a while? I need to go to church."

"I'm glad to. You go ahead." He pulled her into a side hug. "You may want to grab a shower before going to church, Dan. The smell of smoke on you is overbearing."

He nodded. "I need to stop home to feed Sammy and let him out. I'll shower while I'm there."

14

Ashley awakened in a sterile room feeling battered and weary, but alive. She tried to sit up, but it was too much of a struggle, so she gave up and stayed put.

> *Father, I don't know why you allowed me to survive that fire, but you must have something left for me to do here on earth. Show me what it is, so I don't mess up again. Allow me to see your will clearly.*

A nurse bustled past the open door, but didn't come in.

Carly knocked softly to alert Ashley to her presence.

"Come in."

Carly squeezed her hand. "You gave us quite a scare."

"Us?"

"Thomas and me."

"Oh." She scooted back and sat up a little. "Sorry about that."

"You have nothing to be sorry for. Do you remember what happened?"

"I heard a noise downstairs, so I decided to check it out. I recognized the man. He was at the parade with Ivy."

"Wow. I can't imagine what kind of monster would try to murder an innocent woman."

"How did I get here?"

"The EMTs brought you by ambulance."

"I guessed that much. I meant how did they know about the fire. Did someone call it in?"

"You don't remember?"

"Remember what?"

"Danny rescued you."

"Daniel?" She squeaked the name past her scratchy throat. "How?"

"He told me that he was driving past your house when he noticed the door was wide open. At that time of night and with as cold as it was, it didn't sit right with him, so he went inside to check on you. When he did, well, you know what he found."

"Is he here?"

"He stayed beside you through the night, but he left first thing this morning. Muttered something about church."

"Oh. Okay." The thought of Dan going to church lifted her spirits some, but the fact that he was gone, and she might never see him again cut deep. She'd hoped to at least thank him for saving her life before she flew home. "Do you think they'll discharge me?

"Probably. You're awake and seem to be doing well considering." Carly frowned.

"I want to go home. Hopefully, Mr. Harrington will understand if I don't stay until January."

Carly bit her bottom lip. "The police have been hanging around hoping to get your statement as soon as you wake up."

"When you head out would you tell them I'm ready to meet with them?"

"Are you sure?"

"The sooner the better, right?"

"Sure."

꼬

ASHLEY FINGER-combed her hair and tried to look as presentable as possible, so she could talk to the police. Five minutes later, Max showed up. She smiled up at him.

"Hi, Max."

"I thought you might be more comfortable with a familiar face, but if you'd prefer, I can get a female officer to do your interview."

"Nah. I'm glad it's you."

He peppered her with questions. Answering them brought back the previous night in vivid detail leaving her feeling vulnerable all over again.

Max put a hand on her shoulder. "We can get a psychologist or someone from the clergy to come in and see you if you'd like that."

"No. I'll call my pastor back home if I need to talk. I've only been in Freedom a short time, so I didn't develop any strong bonds in the local church."

~

DAN HADN'T gone home yet despite Carly's suggestion to shower. He stared at the side door to Freedom Bible Church wondering if they'd changed the code on the lock since his last visit. So much time had passed, he couldn't be certain. He entered the five digits, and the lock released. He let out a shaky laugh as he opened the door.

He briefly closed his eyes, and sent up a prayer of thanksgiving. A huge weight lifted from his shoulders. How had he let his anger keep him away for so long?

He hurried through the foyer, up the stairs and into the main part of the church where rows of pews were assembled in front of the podium and the altar which held a King James Bible with the AV 1611 text. He'd always admired that Bible.

Making his way down the aisle to the altar, he dropped to his knees and opened his heart to the Lord. Thirty minutes later, he wiped the sweat from his brow and left the way he'd come in. As he closed the door behind him, Pastor Stephenson crossed the parking lot.

"Daniel. It's been a while. Glad you stopped by."

"Hi, Pastor." Dan shifted his weight from one foot to the other.

"You smell like smoke."

"I know."

"Care to talk about it?"

"A close friend was nearly killed in an arson last night. I barely made it in there in time to save her. We both may have died if the fire department hadn't arrived when they did."

"The ladies kept you on their prayer chain." The pastor clapped him on the back. "Something tells me you've needed those prayers."

"I have. Will you thank them for me?"

"Absolutely. You headed out already?"

"I need to go home, shower, and take care of my dog and then get to work, but I'll be here Christmas Eve, Lord willing."

Pastor Stephenson nodded. "I'm glad to hear it. See you then."

~

DAN FINISHED the staff meeting with the kitchen and waitstaff and rushed back to his office to grab his keys from his desk. He wanted to get to the hospital before Ashley was released.

Twenty minutes later he pulled up at the hospital and learned that Ashley had been discharged several hours earlier. The drive to her place took about fifteen minutes, but it seemed longer as he practiced his apology in his head. He pulled onto her street to find several police cars and the fire marshal parked in front of her house. He got out of his truck and made a beeline for the group of men standing by a police car.

Max excused himself from the group when he noticed him. "What are you doing here, Dan?"

"I came to see Ashley."

"She's gone, man."

"What do you mean gone?"

"She booked a flight that was leaving at three o'clock this afternoon." He glanced at his watch. "That means she should be boarding her flight right about now. We weren't able to save much from this wreckage, but her passport was in a fireproof safe, so we were able to rescue it for her. With nothing left here, she was determined to get home."

Dan walked back over to his truck and leaned against it. "She's really gone?"

Max followed. "Carly took her to pick up her cat from the firehouse and then drove her to the airport." He sighed. "You can call, or you can once she gets a new cell phone. She was going to wait until she arrived home to purchase one."

"What am I going to do without her?"

"Aren't you the one who told her to resign?"

Dan scowled.

"Don't look at me that way. Word got around the lodge. Nobody else wanted to see her go. Maybe you should've kept your personal life out of the kitchen."

"Thanks, buddy. Kick me while I'm down, why don't you?"

"I don't mean to do that, Dan, but if this girl meant so much to you that you couldn't face her every day once the two of you had a spat, maybe you should fix whatever went wrong between you. You and Ivy broke up, and it never bothered you to be around her. What's different about Ashley?"

"Everything." He met Max's gaze. "I need to book a flight to Pennsylvania."

"That's the spirit." Max laughed. "Make sure to let Mr.

Harrington and Kevin know you're leaving, okay?"

"I'll call them from Denver International." He pulled a key off his keyring and handed it to Max. "Take care of my dog while I'm gone?"

"Sure. When did you get a dog?"

"In November."

"Does this dog have a name?"

"His name is Sammy. He's friendly."

"Good luck, Dan."

"I don't need luck. I've got Almighty God on my side."

~

ASHLEY HAD no bags to collect when she got off the plane, so she headed outside to the pickup area to wait for her parents to arrive. Seeing them would be the silver lining to the dark cloud that had followed her around the past few days. The traffic was heavy, and the smell of exhaust was thick in the air.

Her father's Lexus pulled up to the curb, and she opened the door. She climbed in behind her mother who turned to greet her. "We're so glad you're home." She inhaled her mother's familiar floral scent, and it comforted her.

"Me too, Mom." She bit her lip and glanced toward her father who pulled out into traffic and merged onto I95.

He met her gaze in the rear-view mirror. "I can't believe your house burned down. Are you sure you're okay? You look like you were in a boxing match."

She sighed. "It was an arson. I came downstairs and caught him in the act, so he beat me up."

Her mother gasped. "Are you telling me someone tried to murder you?!"

"I'm fine, Mom."

"So, it's true. Your house was singled out by an arsonist?"

"I'm home now. I don't know why my rental house was targeted, but the police will handle it." She had her suspicions, but there was no reason to give her parents any more justification for worrying. "I'm too tired to rehash it, do you mind if we change the subject?"

"If that's what you want. Sure." Her mother turned to inspect her once more. "Your sister and her husband returned from a medical conference yesterday. Greg was the keynote speaker."

"That sounds like quite an honor. Did the kids stay with you?"

"Their nanny stayed with them at their house while they were away. Annabelle thought it would be less disruptive to their schedule that way." Ashley thought it would've been nicer for them to be with their grandparents, but kept her opinions to herself. She didn't want to make waves.

When they finally pulled up outside her parents large Victorian home, she breathed a sigh of relief.

THE NEXT flight into Philadelphia didn't leave until eleven o'clock at night. So if his flight's departure was on schedule, he would arrive around midnight Eastern time, and he wouldn't be able to see Ashley until morning. Hanging out at the Denver International Airport to await his flight held little appeal, so he took the sky ride to the Northfield Stapleton Mall to occupy time. Finding a bench, he sat and let his thoughts wander. Since he'd returned from Afghanistan, his life had been empty.

After Ivy's betrayal, he'd thrown himself into work and let his job become his top priority, or at least he had before Ashley bumped into him before her interview. Thinking back at how her eyes had widened at the shock of slamming into him and seeing how she'd steeled herself against the pain from the scalding coffee, it struck him how strong she must be. He'd watched her march into human resources, prepared to interview for the position despite her predicament.

Could any man be immune to her charms? The woman was beautiful, tender-hearted, affectionate, and, most importantly, godly. He'd pushed God from his life, but she'd subtly brought the Lord into nearly every conversation they had. If he'd opened his heart sooner, he might've heard God's gentle voice before everything spiraled out of control. Now he could only hope that Ashley would give him another chance. He had to believe she would forgive him and come back.

Two hours before his flight was scheduled, he made his way back to the airport and checked in. The long night and longer day were wearing on him, but he needed to stay alert enough to board his flight. There was no way he'd miss it and his chance to reconcile things with the woman he loved.

Love. Was that what he felt or was it infatuation? He'd been so sure he loved Ivy, but his heart hadn't been broken when he called off the engagement. His pride had been hurt, but he wasn't crushed. When he'd discovered Ashley had flown back to Pennsylvania he'd been devastated. Yes. It had to be love. There was no other explanation for what he was feeling.

When he finally boarded the plane, he could barely keep his eyes open. The stress caught up with him, and he slept until the captain announced their descent.

15

When they landed at the Philadelphia International Airport, Dan waited for the other passengers to deplane, so as not to get caught up in the mass of people. Crowds made him nervous since he'd returned home from the Middle East. He followed the signs for the baggage claim hoping they'd lead him out of the building. They did. Competing odors of gasoline, tar, and factory fumes surrounded him as he stepped outside. There was no line of taxis waiting, so he ordered an Uber from his cell phone. While he waited, he called Sabrina to request Ashley's emergency contact address. He hadn't remembered to look it up before leaving the office.

Ten minutes later a man pulled up in a Volkswagen Jetta and he got in. "Do you know where I can find a nice hotel to stay for the night in Delaware County?"

"There are some decent motels in that area, but the best hotels are in Center City or here at the airport."

"Decent will be fine." He gave the driver the address he'd gotten from Sabrina. "Somewhere near this address would be perfect."

Thirty-five minutes later, he was checking into the Hilton Garden Inn on Route 3 in Newtown Square. He let himself into the room and forced himself to lie down and rest. He couldn't go look for Ashley until daybreak.

When morning arrived, he ordered an Uber and headed down to the first floor. Taking advantage of the breakfast buffet the hotel offered, he grabbed a scone and a coffee and found a seat that allowed him to watch for the arrival of his ride. He tapped his foot and stared out the window. When the car pulled up fifteen minutes later, he hurried outside. After getting in, he gave the address to the driver who took him to a large Victorian style home with a perfectly manicured lawn. He asked the driver to wait and knocked on the front door.

A young woman answered. "May I help you?"

"I hope so. I'm looking for Ashley Castle."

"Sorry. Miss Ashley's not here."

"Do you know where I can find her?"

"I'm not sure I should give out that information."

He sighed. "How about this? I'll give you my cell number. I'm staying at a nearby hotel. Would you tell Ashley I'm in town and ask her to call me?"

The woman nodded.

"Thank you."

He wondered who the young lady was that answered the door. Maybe she worked for Ashley's parents. As soon as he arrived at the hotel, his cell rang.

"Who is this?" asked the voice on the other end.

"You called me. Shouldn't you know who I am?"

"My nanny didn't remember your name. What do you want with my sister-in-law?"

"I'm Ashley's boss. And her friend."

"If that's true, why don't you have her phone number."

"Her cell phone was destroyed in the fire."

"What fire?"

"I'll let her tell you about that. Will you help me get in touch with her or not?"

"What's your name?"

"Daniel Winchester. Please tell her I flew here from Colorado to see her. I won't leave until I do."

"I'll let her know."

Another twenty minutes passed while he paced back in forth in the motel room waiting to hear from Ashley. His cell finally rang. He answered on the first ring.

"Is it true?" Ashley's asked.

"Is what true?"

"Are you here?"

"I am."

"Why?"

"For you, Ash."

"I don't understand." Her voice was barely above a whisper.

"May I see you?"

"Okay." She gave him the address, and he scribbled it down.

"I have to call an Uber, but I'll be there as soon as I can."

It took longer than he expected for the Uber to come. The ride down Goshen Road was like a Sunday drive through the country. It wound past large estates until he they arrived at their destination. They turned down a long driveway which led past barns and a greenhouse. Covered in a fresh layer of snow, the property was breathtaking.

It wasn't at all what he'd expected. He paid the driver and waited for him to leave before walking up to the massive stone door. Ashley answered seconds after he knocked. He took note of the purple bruising under her eyes and the gash across her lip. One side of her face was swollen and discolored. He pulled her to him and hugged her gently.

∾

ASHLEY ACCEPTED Daniel's hug. Her whole body trembled at his touch, so she took a step back and let him enter the foyer. "Why did you show up at my sister's house looking for me?"

"I asked Sabrina for the address of your emergency contact. I didn't ask for a name, so I assumed it was your parents' house."

"My parents often travel outside of the country, so I used my sister as my emergency contact." She blinked a few times and took a step back. "What is this about, Danny? Why are you here?"

"I came to say I'm sorry."

"What are you sorry for? You saved my life."

"I regret everything that happened at the parade and since."

"Nothing that happened was your fault, so I'm not sure what you have to regret."

"Stop." His tone was angry and demanding.

"Stop what?" She whispered. "What did I do now?"

"Please let me say everything I came to say."

"Fine. My parents are in the den, so we'll have more privacy if we sit in the living room." She led the way to an enormous room with formal furniture. She motioned for him to take a seat and sat on the opposite end of the couch leaving enough room for three people between them.

"So, this is your parents' house?"

"It is."

"I didn't realize you came from money."

"I don't advertise it." Her smile wavered when she realized smiling probably made her look even more monstrous. "It's not like it's my money anyway."

"Yeah. I understand that."

"I guess you would." She recalled the elaborate Christmas celebration he'd taken her to at his father's development firm. She'd known he came from a wealthy family, so she wasn't sure why she hadn't told him about her own family. It didn't matter now. "I don't think you came to discuss our parents' financial statuses."

He rubbed the back of his neck. "You're not going to make this easy for me, are you?"

"I don't even know what 'this' is?" She cast a furtive glance his way, as she smoothed invisible wrinkles in her slacks.

"I want you to come back to Colorado."

She gave him a little head shake. "I'm sorry, Danny. I can't do that."

"Why not?"

"My house is gone for one. Plus, I don't think I can work with you, and I definitely can't continue to be your friend."

"Why can't you?" He raked his fingers through his hair. "Was my overreaction so bad that you can't stand to be around me?"

"No. That isn't it."

His eyes shone brightly. "Explain it to me."

"Being close to you is too painful," she whispered.

"Why?" He closed the distance between them on the couch and took her hands in his. "Why would being around me cause you pain?"

Her heart raced at his touch. "My feelings for you are complicated." She snatched her hands away and stood. She saw her own pain reflected in his eyes. "I want more from you, Danny, but I know that isn't possible. I'll show you out."

He stood. "Ash?"

"What?" she asked.

He spun her around to face him and pulled her to him. "Why isn't it possible?"

"You're with Ivy." She pushed him away.

"I am not."

"I walked in on you and Ivy one day when you were in a banquet room. Her arms were looped around your neck and her fingers were in your hair. It sure looked like you'd reconciled with her."

"Ashley, I'm sorry. I didn't realize you'd walked in on that. I would've gone to find you immediately after I'd extricated myself from her embrace. I told her I wasn't interested in rekindling our romance. It wasn't the first time she tried. She comes onto me frequently, but I don't welcome her advances."

"Honestly?"

"You are the only woman I have eyes for these days."

He pulled her close and leaned his forehead against hers. "I didn't come here to ask the Liberty Grille's chef to return to work."

"You didn't?"

"I came here to bring you home to me."

"You have feelings for me?"

"How could you doubt that for a second? I come up with reasons to be around you. I asked you to plan my father's birthday celebration despite having a capable administrative assistant and a lodge event planner I could ask. When you're at work, I'm there. When I have to be somewhere else, I ask you to join me."

"I hadn't thought about it like that."

Her insides turned to mush as he lowered his lips to hers, and he kissed her gently but with urgency and desire. "I've wanted to do that since the moment you caused me to spill my coffee on the day we met." He leaned away but kept his hands on her waist. The contact sent tiny electric shocks all the way to her toes. "Your injuries must be painful, and I don't want to hurt you."

Leaning into him, she pulled him back down to her and kissed him. "My injuries are the last thing on my mind."

"Will you please come back to Colorado?"

"I don't think I can." She took a step back.

"Why not? I thought you cared for me, too."

"What if you get bored with me and change your mind? Where will that leave me? I'll have to leave Freedom Ridge again, and I'll be back home with my parents explaining to them why I'm once again a complete failure at life and a major disappointment to them."

"You are not a failure at anything. You're an excellent chef who could have her pick of restaurants." He placed his hands on her shoulders. "Why would you think I would change my mind?"

"You broke up with Ivy. She's a ten. I'm a six on my best day."

"You're every bit as beautiful as Ivy, but your heart is tender and kind. Don't compare yourself to Ivy or any other woman. There is no comparison. You are a far better woman than any other I've known. I could never get bored with you."

She cocked her head to the side. "Why did you two breakup?"

"I broke the engagement after she spent the night with my best-friend, Gage, when he was injured and came home to recover."

"I had no idea." She leaned toward him and put a hand on his arm.

"It's not something I share with many people."

"That explains the animosity between you and Gage." She bit the inside of her cheek. "Why did you hire Ivy to work at Liberty Grille after she'd betrayed you?"

"She needed a job. There aren't many employers in a small town like Freedom and waiting tables is all she knows how to do. Valentino's and Evelyn's refused to hire her after what happened. I think they were astonished when I did."

"I'll bet.

"What happens if I come back to Colorado?"

"It's probably too soon to say for sure, but give us a chance. I promise you my feelings for you are real, and I know you must feel the intensity of my emotions when we kiss." He brushed a stray hair behind her ear and caressed the sensitive skin beneath her ear with his thumb.

"How can you be so sure?" She whispered.

"Have a little faith, Ashley. You trust God with everything else, why not trust Him with this?"

A tentative smile graced her lips. "You make a persuasive argument. Okay."

"Okay, what?"

"I'll come back with you to Colorado."

He kissed her again, and she lost herself in his kiss. Once they parted, he gazed into her eyes, and she saw the depth of her own feelings reflected in his. He pulled her into a hug. She winced, and he backed off. "I'm sorry. I keep forgetting you're injured."

"I don't know how you can forget when I look like a monster."

"You're as beautiful as ever. Inside and out."

～

DAN STRAIGHTENED his tie. The shoulders of the borrowed tux were snug, but the pant length fit, so he'd make-do. He felt like an idiot. What would he say to Ashley's parents? Would they think him a love-sick fool to have traveled from Colorado to convince their daughter to come back? It didn't matter if they did. He'd done the right thing.

Having found her, he couldn't live without her. He'd considered proposing, but it was too soon. They'd spent time a lot of time together, but mostly as friends. When he was ready to ask her, he'd ask his mother for his great-grandmother's ring. He hadn't used it to propose to Ivy because the diamond was minuscule. He'd been afraid Ivy would scoff at anything less than a carat since she knew he had a huge trust fund he could tap into. Ashley wasn't like that. She'd love the history his great-grandmother's ring represented.

Driving back to Goshen Road to meet her, he mulled over his options.

He stood at her front door feeling like a teenager picking up his prom date when her father answered. "Come in. The women are nearly ready. I have a car picking us up to take us into the city."

"Thank you, sir." Dan shifted from one foot to the other. "I appreciate your coming up with an extra ticket for me."

"It wasn't a problem. A simple phone call took care of it." Mr. Castle moved into the formal living room and Dan followed. "Care for a drink?"

"No. I'm fine, sir." He eyed the stairs hoping Ashley

would join them soon.

"Enough with the 'sir'."

"What would you like me to call you, Mr. Castle?"

"Henry will do fine."

"Okay, sir, I mean Henry."

He heard footsteps on the staircase and looked up in time to see Ashley descending the stairs in a gorgeous floor length fitted black gown. She'd applied makeup to cover her bruises. The effect was stunning. If they'd been alone, he would've been tempted to do more than admire her.

~

ONCE THE awkwardness between Daniel and her parents passed, the night went smoothly.

Dan held her hand as they sat at the ballet watching the Nutcracker. Afterward, he was attentive and friendly at the after party held for patrons of the ballet. He assimilated to her parents' world far more harmoniously than she did. Conformity wasn't her strong suit. She found it preferable to keep to herself than to make small talk with acquaintances and strangers.

Dan came up beside her and placed a hand on her elbow. "Is everything okay?"

"Yes. Fine."

"You aren't having fun, are you?"

"That obvious?"

"It's clear this isn't your scene." He smiled. "We may

need to attend these types of events from time to time to appease our parents, but it won't be so bad if we attend them together."

She ran her fingers along the lapels of his jacket. "Spending time with you isn't so painful."

"Let's dance." He placed his hand on her elbow and guided her to the dance floor. She matched his steps as he waltzed her across the floor.

Being in his arms eased her discomfort, and she felt safe and protected. Home was no longer a renovated farmstead in Newtown Square. Home was wherever Daniel was. Her heart was his to do with as he wished. She sent up a prayer that God would allow their relationship to flourish.

16

Dan paced outside his office door. Ashley returned to Colorado with him and would stay in the lodge until Margie, her real estate agent, found her a new place to rent. He worked it out with Kevin that morning. The one thing he couldn't figure out was how to ensure her safety.

How could he protect her against an enemy he didn't recognize? The face was familiar, but with the grainy image from the camera, he wasn't certain the experts could identify him. He'd soon find out though. While he'd been in Pennsylvania, Max had reviewed the footage Heath had given him. According to Max, it was being run through facial recognition software, but there were no hits yet. All he could do was wait, but he was no good at waiting.

"Dan?"

"What is it, Sabrina?"

His dark-haired assistant smoothed her braid over her shoulder and stood in his path. "Stop."

"Stop what?"

"Whatever it is you're doing. Go home and get some rest."

"I just got here."

"You've been here for four hours and you came directly from the airport." She put her hands on her hips. "Get out of here. Pacing will not help you get answers any faster. It's Christmas Eve. Go home." He glanced at his watch. If they left now, they could make it to Christmas Eve service.

"Okay. You win." He stepped into his office to grab his stuff and waved to Sabrina on his way past her desk. "I'd forgotten it was Christmas Eve. You go home, too. Enjoy the holiday weekend with your son, and I'll see you Monday morning."

He pushed the kitchen door open, and all activity stopped. "What's going on in here?"

Carly grinned. "Nothing."

"Nothing?"

Ashley laughed and handed a roasting pan to Carly. "Get back to work while I chat with the boss."

"He's the boss here, but who is the boss when you're away from work?" Thomas snickered.

"Stop that! Keep in mind, we're both your bosses when you're here, so you shouldn't annoy either one of us." Ashley rubbed her hands over her face. Looking up at him, she shook her head. "Sorry."

"What for?" He reached for her hand and pulled her around the counter to him. He lifted her chin and stared into her eyes before kissing her in front of the staff. "Care to go to Christmas Eve service with me?"

"I'm working."

"The boss gave you the rest of the night off." He looked

over at Carly. "Can you handle things here?"

"Sure thing, boss," Carly said.

"In that case, I'd love to join you." She placed her hand in his.

~

THEY SNUCK into the back of Freedom Bible Church and sat in the last pew as the pastor made his way to the podium. The sermon focused on the shepherds who were visited by the Angel of the Lord and directed to the babe in the manger.

After the sermon several people got up to sing Christmas specials, and she lost herself in the beautiful music.

Ashley felt complete. Complete in the Lord, but also satisfied knowing the man she loved was beside her. She laced her fingers with Danny's and slid closer to him. It was a relief to know that her attraction for him hadn't been one-sided. If she'd known how he felt when she'd boarded that flight, she wouldn't have left, but she was glad she did, since it forced his hand, and he'd come for her.

Having him show up at her parents' house and express his desire for her to return said more than mere words ever could. He hadn't told her he loved her, but she hadn't said the words either. It was too early in their relationship for her to make herself that vulnerable.

The pastor asked them to form a circle around the pews, and they sang silent night with only candles lighting the room. The pastor said a prayer and Church let out.

They spent a few minutes greeting their brothers and sisters in Christ before Dan leaned down to whisper in her ear.

"I'm not ready to take you back to the lodge. I think we both need some relaxation."

"What did you have in mind?"

"A movie?"

"At the movie theater or your place?"

"I'd prefer my place, but whichever you'd like."

"I'd rather avoid crowds."

"My place it is."

―

ASHLEY WASN'T sure why she'd agreed to be alone with Dan. Unsupervised time alone in his house was downright dangerous to her self-control. He pulled her close to him on the couch, and the spicy scent of his cologne tickled her nose. Her head told her distance was her friend, but her heart was thrilled by his affection.

"Danny, we need to be careful."

He pointed the remote at the television and hit the pause button. "Careful of what?"

"You know what I mean."

He leaned in for a kiss. "I promise not to take advantage of you, but I need to reassure myself that you're here beside me." He sighed. "I can't stop picturing you surrounded by flames. And when I think of what could've happened if I hadn't arrived when I did…"

"I know." She held him and ran her hands up and down his back enjoying the feel of his corded muscles beneath her fingers. "After the parade when I realized how deeply I'd hurt you and thought our relationship couldn't be mended, I was devastated."

"I'm sorry I put you through that."

"I brought it on myself."

"No you didn't. You'd gone to Heath and Max. I simply hadn't realized that. Even once I did, I didn't want to forgive you. I didn't understand why you hadn't come to me, but then I realized I hadn't given you reason to trust me. Heath pulled up video of Ivy and Sean from the day Thomas started."

"And?"

"It wasn't the only thing on the video."

"Her hands covered her face."

"The guilt tore me up when I realized I'd caused you to cry."

"You weren't supposed to see that."

He took her hands in his and lifted them to his lips. "I hope I never make you cry again."

"I wouldn't count on that. When you're invested in another person, pain is a part of the equation. People are only human, and they hurt each other. Often unintentionally."

"You're a wise woman."

"I'm sorry I didn't come to you right away."

"All is forgiven." He gave her a tiny smile. "Now I need you to forgive me for making you cry."

She laughed. "I did that weeks ago."

"I'm so thankful to have you here with me."

"Me too." She let out a contended sigh. "It feels like a dream."

～

CHRISTMAS MORNING came with a dusting of fresh white powder covering everything. Dan stared out his kitchen window at the snow-covered peaks and smiled. It would be his first Christmas with Ashley. They'd spend it at work, of course, but afterward he hoped they'd have private time to enjoy each other's company. For now, he needed to pick up Ashley and head over to his parents' house. He'd promised his mother that they'd join them for brunch.

Ashley came to the door of her hotel room dressed in a black skirt that flared out at the bottom and a red blouse.

He smiled. "You look amazing."

"Shall we go?"

"In a hurry to get this over with?"

"Not at all. I like your parents. This will be fun."

He grinned. "Everything is so uncomplicated with you."

"Shouldn't it be?"

He caught her around the waist and pulled her to him nuzzling her neck as he did. "I want you to know how much it means to me that you came back."

She turned in his arms and met his gaze. Her arms looped around his neck, and he kissed her. She shivered reminding him that it was too cold to keep her outside. He opened the passenger door for her before climbing into the driver's seat. "We'll be a little late this morning, but the breakfast chef agreed to stay late, and Carly and Thomas should have the kitchen under control."

"How far do your parents live?"

"About ten minutes from here. Their property is secluded. I think you'll like it."

They arrived at his parents' house, and he opened the door for Ashley and placed his hand on the small of her back to guide her to the kitchen door where he always entered.

His mother looked up from her paper when he entered. "Daniel, why didn't you bring your guest in through the front door?"

"It was unnecessary." He shook his head. "Mother, you've met Ashley."

"I have. Nice to see you again, Ashley. Welcome."

"Thank you, Mrs. Winchester. You have a lovely home."

"I'm glad Daniel was able to convince you to return to Colorado."

"Mother." His tone held a warning. The last thing he needed was for his mother to embarrass Ashley when she'd been gracious enough to join him for Christmas with his parents.

"Would you care for some coffee, Ashley?"

"That would be wonderful. Thank you."

His mother moved to the Keurig and quickly brewed Ashley a mug of coffee. "Cream and sugar?"

"Yes, please. Both."

His mother spooned in two teaspoons of sugar and added some cream. He wasn't used to seeing her play hostess. She usually let him or his sister take the role when there was no hired help around. He smiled to himself as he watched her hand Ashley the cup.

"Thank you."

"You're welcome."

As he'd expected, brunch was catered. His mother ushered them into the dining room where the table was covered with enough food to feed two dozen people despite the fact that there were only four of them in attendance.

"Everything looks delicious," Ashley said.

His father cleared his throat. "Say grace, Dan."

He did so thanking God for the bountiful blessings of food and fellowship. All too soon, the meal was over, and they had to rush out the door to get to the restaurant.

"Thank you so much for having me," Ashley said as the two of them left.

ASHLEY WASN'T sure what to make of Dan's quiet demeanor on the ride to work. She couldn't help but think that he might be having second thoughts. She wondered if she'd said or done something wrong.

"You're awfully quiet."

"Sorry. My mind is back at my parents' house." He sighed. "I haven't mentioned it before because I didn't want to worry you, but Max got the results back from the dinnerware he tested after Dad's birthday party."

"And?"

"The crab was only on my father's glass. It wasn't something we serve in the kitchen. Dad was intentionally poisoned."

"Someone tried to kill your father?"

"They probably thought he'd have an EpiPen, but they certainly intended to scare me."

"You're worried they'll try again."

"First my dad, then you, who will be next?" His eyes were glassy.

She reached over and took his hand in her own and kissed his knuckles. "I'm sorry this is happening to you."

"I should be the one who is sorry. If I hadn't fallen for you, you probably wouldn't have been targeted by a madman."

"I wouldn't choose safety over you."

"That's why I'm afraid." He turned into the lodge parking lot and drove around to the Liberty Grille. "Promise me you'll watch your back when I'm not with you?"

"God is watching over me, Daniel."

He sighed. "You're right. I need to exercise some faith."

"We both do."

"You're good for me." He leaned over and kissed her gently on the lips. "I hadn't realized how empty my life was before you came into it."

17

Dan glanced at the clock on his office wall. It was only six-thirty, and they wouldn't be closing until nine, so the restaurant remained filled to capacity with holiday revelers. A knock on his door captured his attention. "Come in."

The door opened to reveal his assistant dressed to the nines. "Sabrina?"

She smiled.

"What are you doing here?"

"Merry Christmas to you, too, Danny."

"Merry Christmas." He grinned. "I meant, what brings you in on your day off."

"I have family staying at the lodge, so my mom made reservations to have Christmas dinner here so we wouldn't have to spend all day in the kitchen."

"Smart woman."

Sabrina walked up to his desk and straightened a pile of papers. "The food was delicious. Ashley outdid herself."

"I'll come out with you, and you can introduce me to your

family." He grinned. "I'd love to meet your son."

"You don't have to do that."

"I want to."

"Danny?"

"Yeah?"

"Why do you have a picture of Carly's boyfriend on your desk?"

"I don't."

She picked up the grainy photograph and flicked the man in it. "Yes. You do. This is Carly's boyfriend, Sean."

He felt his heart race. Carly had requested the night off last minute. Was she with that madman? "You're sure?"

"I am."

"That's the man who tried to kill Ashley."

The color drained from Sabrina's face. "Carly's with him now. She texted me last night that they were going to his cabin to spend Christmas."

"I know it's your day off, but would you mind getting Heath while I call Max?"

"I'm on it." Sabrina hurried off down the hall.

He picked up the telephone on his desk and called Max's cell number. He answered on the first ring.

"We have a problem." He explained the situation to his friend, and once he'd done that, he called Carly's brother. He hated to do it, but Gage needed to know his sister was in danger.

It took him three rings to pick up. "Gage here."

"It's Dan."

"What's up, Danny?"

"Your sister is in trouble."

"What? What do you mean trouble? What kind of trouble?"

"You know that fire at our chef's house a few days ago?"

"I heard about it."

"The man who set it took your sister to a cabin somewhere."

"Why would she go with him?"

"Long story. Why don't you come in, and we'll meet and strategize how best to find her and get her to safety?"

"I'll be there in ten minutes."

His next stop was the kitchen. So much for a peaceful Christmas with Ashley by his side. Guilt gnawed at his gut for even thinking about his own needs at a time like this.

He pushed through the kitchen door and made eye contact with Ashley. She set down the spatula she'd been using and moved to him silently. Unasked questions burned in her eyes. "Let's go outside."

She followed without a word. He stopped at the locker room and picked up her coat. "You may need this."

She nodded.

He held the door for her. "I've got something I need to tell you."

"What is it? I sensed something was wrong the moment I saw your face."

"The man who tried to kill you has Carly."

"What makes you think that?" She frowned. "Carly went away with her boyfriend. They've been seeing each other since early November when he rear-ended her car."

"Sabrina met him. She saw the picture in my office of the man from the security video and asked me why I had Carly's boyfriend's picture on my desk."

"Oh no." Ashley put her face in her hands. "I had no idea. He's picked her up here numerous times, but she always meets him in the lobby, and I'm usually still in the kitchen when she leaves."

"This isn't your fault."

"Isn't it?" She let out a bitter laugh. "If I hadn't run home to Pennsylvania, we might've had a chance to discover who he was before she left with him."

He stood and pulled her into his arms. "We'll get her back. For now we need to go back inside. Gage will be here soon, so we need to set up in a conference room and figure out how to find her."

They separated and he held her hand until they reached the door by his office. He opened it and held it until she entered.

Heath rushed toward them. "Sabrina told me. Do we have a plan?"

"I called Max. He's alerting the rest of the force, and he'll meet us here." He sighed. "I also called Gage. He'll be here any second if he isn't already."

ASHLEY LOOKED around at the faces of the others assembled at the conference room table. Her short fingernails bit into her skin because she held her fists so tightly. She forced her hands to relax and attempted to smooth out the indentations that remained in her palms.

Gage glared at her, and she felt deserving of his fury. How had she not known? She should've met Carly's boyfriend. She'd never even asked Carly to see a picture of her and her boyfriend? What kind of friend was she?

The other faces around the table were not as unfriendly. Ivy came into the room and took the seat beside her. She was surprised when the other woman put her hand on top of hers and squeezed. Was it guilt for her involvement that had her showing sympathy and support now? She couldn't know for sure, but she didn't recoil from Ivy. If the woman was remorseful and wanting to help, it wouldn't be wise to turn her away.

"Here's what we have so far…" Officer Harrison put the picture of Sean on the board and started listing what they knew about him. If Sean was even his real name. Everyone yelled out what they knew.

"He drinks pumpkin lattes with extra sugar," Casey said. "What? It's the only thing I know about the dude. He comes in late after the Liberty Grille closes, but before we close. His regular order is a pumpkin latte with extra sugar."

Max narrowed his eyes at the people gathered around the table. "No detail is too small. Thank you, Casey."

"Carly said he was from Texas," Gage said.

"That's what he told me, too," Ivy said.

"Did he say where in Texas?"

"A little town about 50 miles from Fort Bliss," Ivy answered.

"Fort Bliss?" Dan asked. "That's where I did my two-weeks this year." Dan's face blanched. "That's where I've seen him before. The food truck. The one we shut down. He was the owner. How did I not put this together sooner?"

"Out of context it's difficult." Max put a hand on his shoulder. "Are you sure it's the same guy?"

"No. I can't be certain, but the face has been nagging at me, and the connection fits." He sighed. "I need to call my Lieutenant and find out who this guy is." Dan picked up his cell and stepped out of the conference room.

Gage stood. "I might have something that can help."

"What's that?" Max asked.

"The phone Carly carries. It's GPS enabled."

"That's good. We'll need a warrant to track the GPS location, and that will take some time, but we can get the process started." He sighed.

"I don't need a warrant. Her phone is on my plan and she agreed to enable the tracking for her own safety. We didn't expect to need it, but decided it was worth the monthly fee in case we ever did. We can use the tracking service to find her phone. With any luck, when we find her phone, we'll find her."

Dan came back in. "I left a message for him."

Sabrina made eye contact with Danny. "We're going to

track her with her cell. Gage has an app on it." She kicked her high heels off by the door and rushed out of the room. She returned a minute later with a laptop. Sitting down beside Gage, she opened the computer and asked him for login information for his cellular service provider. Another two minutes and she had a location. "It's not far from here. Twenty minutes."

Max looked over her shoulder at the screen. "There are no cabins near there."

"What is out that way?" Gage asked.

"You don't want to know. I need to hurry." Max made eye contact with Gage and then Dan. "Don't follow me. Stay here. Both of you." He turned to Heath. "Keep an eye on them."

Ashley noted that he didn't order her to stay. She glanced at her watch. It was closing time, so Thomas would be fine, not that she would do anything differently even if it inconvenienced him. As soon as Max left, and Daniel and Gage were deep in conversation she slipped away. She'd written down the coordinates she'd seen on Sabrina's screen. Once she buckled her seatbelt, she entered them on her cell and told the device to take her there.

18

Sean watched Carly in the passenger seat beside him as she brought up a navigation app on her cell. He couldn't let her do that. Reaching across the console, he snatched the phone from her hand, rolled down his window, and tossed it.

Her door flung open. She jumped.

He slammed on the brakes and cursed. He parked and got out of his car.

The darkness was thick, but he could make out a shape in the distance.

He picked his way across the snow-covered expanse. Reaching the wounded creature, he asked, "Did you think you could escape me?"

He pulled her to her feet and yanked her to him. "I made you mine. You'll stay mine. Even if it means you have to die. My wife left, but now she's dead."

Carly fought him. Her nails dug into his skin. He cursed when she bit him.

"Walk. It'll be poetic to leave a little piece of trash like you in the landfill, won't it?" He forced her to walk ahead of him and pushed her when she slowed her pace.

She scrambled out of his reach. He caught her by the hair and threw a punch. Her cry rent the night. He hit her again. Soon she'd be unrecognizable.

He forced her to walk again. They'd gone far enough. Out of sight of the road. He pushed her down and pinned her beneath him. The faint sound of sirens reached him. He stopped and listened. They were coming closer. He struggled to his feet and kicked her in the gut one last time. There was no time to finish the job. He hurried to his Charger and sped away.

―

WHEN ASHLEY arrived at the landfill the police were already there. Sirens blasted all around her, and coyotes howled somewhere nearby. She drove past the scene. If she parked up the road maybe the cops wouldn't notice her, and she'd be able to track the exact location of Carly's cell. She pulled off the road and parked in the shadows.

The smell of rotting garbage assaulted her and she pulled her scarf over her nose. She found a deer path and followed it. Her phone beeped, and she knew she was nearing her destination. She stopped in her tracks as an officer scooped up Carly's cell before she could reach for it. "Hey! We found her," the officer yelled.

"No. I'm not Carly. I'm her friend."

"False alarm!" The officer shouted, and grimaced. "What are you doing near the victim's phone?"

"Don't call her a victim. She has a name."

"What are you doing here?"

"I saw the GPS coordinates when Sabrina brought them up on the computer. I came to check on her."

"You're interfering with an investigation, and—"

Max walked up and put his hand on the other officer's arm. "Ashley, I distinctly remember telling everyone to stay put."

"No. You told Gage and Daniel to stay put."

"I must've thought you'd have the sense to stay without a reminder."

"Carly needs me."

"She might, so don't go getting yourself killed. You won't do her any good then, will you?"

A scream pierced the night. Ashley ran toward it.

Max grabbed her arm. "Stay." He motioned for the other officer to come back. "Put her in the back of my car. I'll get her after we check out the scene."

Ashley went with the officer against her will and sat in the back of Max's police car. They didn't handcuff her or even shut the door, but she knew that she'd be stopped if she tried to flee. She watched the officers' flashlights moving farther away from her as they searched for Carly. More than forty-five minutes passed before Max came back to the car. He was smiling. "We found her, Ashley. She's going to live."

"Is she hurt?"

"Come on. You can ride in the ambulance. I'm sure they'll make an exception to their family only rule at my request."

"Thank you."

When she reached the ambulance, Carly lay still. She was caked with blood, but she was awake.

Ashley jumped into the back and took Carly's hand in her own. "I'm sorry I let this happen."

"Not your fault." Carly squeezed her hand. "I shouldn't have gone off with him like that. I felt down to my bones that something was wrong, but I ignored the feeling. I wanted to believe him. He said such pretty words and made me believe he was in love with me. I'm a fool."

"Believing in love doesn't make you a fool."

"It sure feels like it does." Carly closed her eyes. "My head is pounding."

"I'm sure they'll give you something for it at the hospital."

An EMT leaned in close. "I'm Carson. I'm going to be with you until we get to the hospital. We'll start an IV now. The fluids may help take the edge off your headache."

"Thank you." Carly tried to sit up, but he put his hand on her to keep her in place.

"You were beat up pretty badly. Try to be still so we can check the extent of your injuries," Carson said.

"Most of my injuries are from jumping out of the car."

"You did what?"

The ambulance pulled away. Ashley noticed a police escort leave behind them.

"Sean took my cell right out of my hand and tossed it out the window. We were arguing about how to get to the cabin he rented. He said it was on Hidden Lake. I know how to get to

Hidden Lake since I've been going there my whole life. Gage and Danny used to play ice hockey there when they were teenagers. I followed them everywhere."

Ashley gave Carly an encouraging smile, hoping she would continue to share the details of her ordeal. "When he snatched my cell out of my hand, alarm bells went off. I opened the door and jumped. He wasn't going too fast, but it was fast enough that I was stunned when I hit the ground. Seconds later, he'd turned the car around and was searching for me. I tried to hide, but with my injuries, I didn't make it far. He found me and well, you can figure out the rest."

"He beat you?"

"Pummeled me with his fists and kicked me in my ribs." They hit a bump in the road, and Carly winced.

"He didn't?" She couldn't bring herself to come right out and ask if her friend had been violated.

"No. Not that." Ashley was grateful Carly understood without her having to say the words.

"What made him stop?"

"The sirens. When the sirens started, he ran off."

"I hope they can find him."

"Why do you think he did this to me?"

"I'm not entirely sure, but it appears to have something to do with Dan shutting down his business on base at Fort Bliss."

"He did mention something about a soldier ruining his life. He said his wife left him and took the kids after the soldier filed something or other."

"The soldier was Danny Winchester and the something or

other was paperwork which would prevent him from operating his food truck on the base."

"When he lost his income source, his wife ran off."

"My guess is she had more reasons than one."

"It seems he has a penchant for beating women, so that is a distinct possibility. I sure know how to pick them, don't I?"

"Nothing that happened was your fault."

"Except for being so naive I believed every lie he told."

"You were brave to jump out of a moving car. I'm not sure I would've had the courage."

"I wasn't sure if he was a serial killer or something. We were supposed to go one place and he was going in the other direction. I was petrified."

"I'm grateful you're okay."

"Who is running the restaurant if you're here?"

"It was past closing when I left the lodge, but while we were figuring out how to find you, I guess it was Thomas. I don't know for sure and I don't care much. I suppose Thomas and Van handled things in my absence."

"By themselves?"

"They have to learn sometime. It's their trial by fire, I guess." She cringed as the cliche came out, and she thought of the fire that haunted her nightmares every time she closed her eyes.

"Ashley?"

"Yeah?"

"Thanks for being here."

∽

SEAN FLOORED the gas pedal. He could outrun the cops in his Challenger. After a few strategic turns, he pulled into a dirt drive.

He waited for the sirens to pass by. Ten minutes passed. He'd lost them for sure.

It was time to head back to Texas. There was too much heat in Colorado despite the cold temperatures.

∽

DAN LOOKED around the conference room and realized Ashley was gone. He'd check the kitchen and see if she was in there helping Thomas. He didn't think she would've gone home with Carly missing.

Gage was standing at the window, his shoulders were slumped. He raked his hand through his hair and sighed. He walked up to his former friend and put a hand on his shoulder. "They'll bring her back."

"Alive?" Gage asked.

"I believe so with every fiber of my being."

"How did I let this happen? I should've done a background check on the guy dating my sister."

"That isn't normal. Regular people don't do background checks on their siblings suitors. This isn't your fault."

"Why do I feel like it is?"

"We should pray."

"Together?"

ELLE E. KAY

"Yeah. Let's go into my office for some privacy."

Dan walked behind Gage until they reached the privacy of his office. He shut the door behind them.

> *Father, you know where Carly is and who she's with. We ask a hedge of protection around her. Please keep her alive and bring her back to us. Lord, while I have your ear, please heal the relationship between me and Gage so that we can be there for each other the way we used to be. I ask for a forgiving and merciful spirit. Please remove the bitterness from my heart, and help me to fully recommit myself to you.*
>
> *I ask you to strengthen Carly that she may be able to bear what has come her way this night.*
>
> *Please, Lord, let this draw her closer to you and not push her farther away.*
>
> *In Jesus' name I pray, Amen.*

"It's not the way I would've chosen to get you to forgive me, but thanks."

"I'm working on it. Your coming to me the night before the parade got me thinking. I knew I needed to get past my animosity, but couldn't figure out how.

"You reminded me how simple it was. I needed to turn back to God." He stood. "But right now, I'm focused on Carly. I'm going to go and find Ashley. Care to join me?"

"Nah. I think I'll go back to the conference room and see if anyone's heard anything."

"I'll catch up with you in a few."

Dan hurried into the kitchen, but found only Thomas and two dishwashers. The rest of the staff had cleared out. "Have you seen Ashley?"

"She left here with you a couple of hours ago. I haven't seen her since."

"That's strange. She disappeared from the conference room." He sighed. "You don't think she would've tried to find Carly on her own, do you?"

"Doubtful."

∽

DAN RECEIVED the news that Ashley was with Carly. Max called Heath to update him, and he'd shared the news with the rest of them. He parked and glanced over at his passenger who was bouncing his leg up and down impatiently. "Don't forget what Heath said. She's badly injured, so don't let the shock show on your face when you see her. You don't want her to think she's repulsive."

"I was by your side in the Helmand Province, Danny." He had his hand on the door handle. "I've seen my share of disfigured soldiers.

"I wish you hadn't been. Nobody should've lived that nightmare." He sighed. "This is different. It's your sister. Don't expect your reaction to be the same. I'm glad Ashley was unconscious when I first sat with her in the hospital."

"I'll school my features."

The two of them made their way inside. Gage walked to the reception desk while he went to Ashley who was pacing the waiting room in the emergency department. He held his arm out to her, and she tucked herself up close to him. Holding her close, he kissed the top of her head. "You shouldn't have left without saying something to me." He sighed. "I was worried you'd done something foolish like try to find Carly on your own. I see I wasn't wrong."

Her watery eyes looked up to him. "I couldn't let her face this alone. She needed me."

"You're a good friend to her." He squeezed her tighter. "I'm glad you're safe."

"Max made me wait in a squad car."

"He's a good man. Remind me to thank him."

―

AFTER DRIVING through the night, Sean could no longer keep his eyes open. He was about two hours from the New Mexico/Texas border. It wasn't much farther to home, but sleep would claim him soon, and he didn't want to be driving when that happened. He pulled into a cheap motel and rented a room.

When he woke, he continued on his way, and two hours later drove up his street, but saw his house was surrounded by police. They'd figured out who he was. He needed a plan.

Driving on, he merged onto I10. He hadn't driven five minutes when he saw police lights behind him. He floored it, but a big rig changed lanes and before he could switch again, another rig blocked him in and prevented him from escape.

He was pinned.

The tractor trailer in front of him slowed, and he was

forced to do the same.

When he came to a stop there were cops everywhere with guns drawn.

He raised his hands into the air and lowered to his knees.

An officer cuffed him and threw him in the back of a squad car.

∼

ASHLEY MOVED in slow motion preparing for the day ahead. She didn't normally work on Sundays, so she wasn't familiar with the brunch buffet the restaurant hosted. The breakfast chef offered to stay later than usual and help with Carly's responsibilities, but she'd told him it was unnecessary.

She hoped he'd leave soon, so she could get a moment alone before the rest of the crew arrived.

The door from the back hall opened, and Dan walked in. He planted himself a few feet in front of her.

"Hi." He stuffed his hands in his pocket.

"Hey." She gave him a tiny smile.

"You okay?"

She sighed. "I will be. I'm tired after last night. And I'm grateful Carly will recover from her injuries."

"We'll hire a temp to help out while she's out of work."

"It's probably not necessary."

"I'm going to do it anyway."

He cleared his throat. "I have some news from Max."

"You do?"

"They caught him."

"Really?" Her eyes lit. "Where? How?" She came around the counter and threw herself into his arms.

He filled her in on the details of the arrest in Texas. "Colorado wanted to extradite, so he could face charges here, but Texas had a murder charge because they found his wife buried on his property. It will be a long time before he faces the attempted murder and kidnapping charges in Colorado, but he'll likely spend the rest of his life in prison."

She felt an overwhelming sense of peace. She lifted up a silent prayer. *Thank you, Lord.* "God is good."

"Yes. He is."

19

Ashley was relieved when they finally shut the doors to the restaurant at ten o'clock. The early New Year's revelers had kept the restaurant busy all night. She and Carly had both rushed up to her room to get ready for the ball that had started two hours earlier. Dan's mother was in charge of the New Year's Eve Charity Gala this year, so she'd worked with Haven to make it spectacular. The proceeds would go to support the International Children's Heart Foundation.

Thomas came to the room to collect Carly. She wasn't ready to date yet after her ordeal with Sean, so she'd asked Thomas to accompany her. Ashley's excitement intensified when she heard another knock on her hotel room door. She opened the door to find Dan standing there in full black tie.

"Wow." He held out his hand for hers and brought her hand to his lips. "You look stunning."

"Thank you." She smiled. "You don't look too shabby yourself."

"Ready?"

"Sure am." She slipped on her heels, grabbed her clutch, and followed him out the door.

They got on the elevator, and she felt a charge in the air. When they arrived in the lobby, instead of turning toward the hall that would lead them to the ballroom, Dan placed his hand on the small of her back and guided her toward the roaring fire where they'd sat discussing menu plans back in early November. Memories of his arm moving to the back of the sofa and the havoc his closeness had wreaked on her emotions flooded her mind. He gently tugged her down onto that sofa and got down on one knee in front of her and pulled a velvet box from his pocket.

A gasp escaped as he opened the box.

"Ashley, will you do me the honor of becoming my wife?"

"Yes."

He placed the diamond on her left-hand ring finger, before pulling her into his arms. "I was going to ask next year at the tree lighting ceremony, but I couldn't wait that long. I need you by my side."

"I'm glad you didn't wait."

"Do you think Ginger would mind having a dog friend?"

"She'll adjust."

"Good. I think Sammy will like her." He leaned back so he could see her face. "How soon do you want to get married?"

"If there was a pastor here, I'd say, 'How about now?'"

"I don't think that would please your parents."

"Probably not."

"You ready to head in?"

"Absolutely! I can't wait to show Carly the ring."

"About that… I know it's a small diamond, but my great-grandfather gave it to my great-grandmother, so it has immense sentimental value."

She held up her hand mesmerized by the rainbows of light shining from the diamond. "It's perfect. I adore it."

Epilogue

*A*shley inhaled the scent of gardenias in her bouquet before setting it down on the dressing table. She stepped back to admire her dress in the full-length mirror of her childhood bedroom. Her parents requested they have the wedding in Pennsylvania. Dan and his parents had agreed to their plan.

Her mother had wanted to book an exclusive country club for the event, but she'd convinced her that she'd prefer a simple backyard wedding. The flowers were in full-bloom and her mother's gardens had a warm inviting feel.

The doorbell rang, and she hurried down the stairs lifting her gown as she descended. She arrived as her father let her pastor into the house. Pastor Walsh grinned when he caught sight of her. "You're looking lovely, my dear."

"Thank you, Pastor."

"You might want to head back upstairs though. I'm meeting with your groom to go over his vows. I'll be up to see you in a minute."

She turned and hurried back up the stairs as fast as her dress would allow her.

Her mother appeared in her doorway moments later. "You

look beautiful, darling."

"Thanks, Mom."

"I have something for you. Have a seat at your dressing table."

She did and her mother clasped a string of pearls at her neck. "These were my mother's. She wore them on her wedding day, and I wore them on mine. I thought you might want to continue the tradition. They're yours now, so you can pass them down to your own daughter someday."

The thought of children brought a tear to her eye. She pictured Danny helping the kids build a snowman at the lodge. She hoped she would be able to bear him children of his own.

The pastor came up and went over her vows with her and spent a few minutes reminding her of what it means to be a biblical wife.

Once the time arrived, the soft piano music drifted up to her, and her father held out his arm. She couldn't stop smiling as she descended the stairs on her father's arm and made her way out to the backyard where he would give her away. Her soon-to-be husband stood beside the pastor looking as handsome as ever in his custom-tailored tuxedo. She gazed into his eyes. She could hardly believe that the man standing before her wanted to spend the rest of his life with her, but when he kissed her and sealed their promises, she knew her hero's love was the forever kind.

Ready for the story of wonderful EMT, Carson?

Return to Freedom Ridge in Stranded with the Hero, the fourth book in the Heroes of Freedom Ridge Series.

Her solo adventure leaves her alone for the holidays until her rescuer steps in.

Join in all the fun at our Facebook Reader Group www.facebook.com/groups/freedomridgereaders for sneak peeks, giveaways and tons of Christmas romance fun!

HEROES OF FREEDOM RIDGE SERIES

(Year 1)

Rescued by the Hero (Aiden and Joanna)
Mandi Blake

Love Pact with the Hero (Jeremiah and Haven)
Liwen Y. Ho

(Year 2)

Healing the Hero (Daniel and Ashley)
Elle E. Kay

Stranded by the Hero (Carson and Nicole)
Hannah Jo Abbott

(Year 3)

Reunited with the Hero (Max and Thea)
M.E. Weyerbacher

Forgiven by the Hero (Derek and Megan)
Tara Grace Ericson

(Year 4)
Guarded by the Hero (Heath and Claire)
Mandi Blake

Trusting the Hero (Addison and Ty)
Hannah Jo Abbott

(Year 5)
Believing the Hero (Jan and Pete)
Tara Grace Ericson

ELLE E. KAY

Friends with the Hero (Tuck and Patience)
Jessie Gussman

(Year 6)
Persuaded by the Hero (Bryce and Sabrina)
Elle E. Kay

Romanced by the Hero (Mac and Amy)
Liwen Y. Ho

Books by Elle E. Kay
FAITH WRITES PUBLISHING

Endless Mountain Series:

Shadowing Stella

Implicating Claudia

Chasing Sofie

The Lawkeeper Series (Contemporary):

Lawfully Held

A K-9 LAWKEEPER ROMANCE

Lawfully Defended

A S.W.A.T. LAWKEEPER ROMANCE

Lawfully Guarded

A BILLIONAIRE BODYGUARD LAWKEEPER ROMANCE

The Lawkeeper Series (Historical):

Lawfully Taken

A BOUNTY HUNTER LAWKEEPER ROMANCE

Lawfully Given

A CHRISTMAS LAWKEEPER ROMANCE

Lawfully Promised

A TEXAS RANGER LAWKEEPER ROMANCE

Lawfully Vindicated

A US MARSHAL LAWKEEPER ROMANCE

ELLE E. KAY

Blushing Brides Series:
The Billionaire's Reluctant Bride
The Bodyguard's Fake Bride

Heroes of Freedom Ridge:
Healing the Hero
Persuaded by the Hero

Standalone:
Holly's Noel

Lawfully Held: A K-9 Lawkeeper Romance
THE LAWKEEPERS SERIES

Tall tales. High stakes.

FBI Special Agent Justine Gillespie is better at handling bombs than romantic relationships. She goes to Arizona to manage her mother's affairs and get her settled into a nursing home.

A series of misunderstandings lead to her being arrested.

Officer Brady Hall's life changes when he pulls Justine over. She has explanations for everything, but they're not very believable.

When a serial bomber kicks up some chaos, Brady and Justine set their differences aside for the greater good. But will their efforts be enough to save countless lives?

Lawfully Held is now available.

Go to books2read.com/u/bPKPoR for links to retailers.

About The Author

Elle E. Kay lives in Central Pennsylvania. She loves life in the country on her hobby farm with her husband, Joe. Elle is a born-again Christian with a deep faith and love for the Lord Jesus Christ. She desires to live for Him and to put Him first in everything she does.

She writes children's books under the pen-name Ellie Mae Kay.

You can connect with Elle on her website and blog at https://www.elleekay.com/ or on social media:

Facebook: www.facebook.com/ElleEKay7

Pinterest: www.pinterest.com/elleekay7/

Amazon Author Central:

www.amazon.com/author/ellekay

Instagram: www.instagram.com/elleekay7/

Goodreads:

www.goodreads.com/author/show/15016833.Elle_E_Kay

Note to Reader

DEAR READER,

I hope you enjoyed reading my novel, *Healing the Hero.* If you did, check out some of my other titles. For a list of my current books and upcoming releases check out the novel page on my website: https://www.elleekay.com/novels/.

I'd love it if you'd sign up for my newsletter at https://www.elleekay.com/newsletter-sign-up/.

If you enjoyed *Healing the Hero*, the most helpful thing you can do is leave an honest review. So, please consider submitting a review with the retailer where you purchased this book. It doesn't cost anything other than a moment of your time and can be tremendously beneficial to me. Your quick review helps to get my book into the hands of other readers who may enjoy it.

https://readerlinks.com/mybooks/2115/1/7804

Thank you.
Elle E. Kay
https://www.elleekay.com

Acknowledgements

Thanks go out to the other five authors writing for the Heroes of Freedom Ridge series. I'm happy to be a part of this special series that I'm sure you'll love. Thank you, ladies, for taking the time to beta read for me.

A special thank you to my editor, Patti Geesey, who always does a remarkable job of helping me polish my work.

I'd also like to extend my thanks to you, my readers. Without your support, I wouldn't be able to earn a living sharing clean and wholesome stories for Christians. It is my prayer that my books touch hearts and draw souls closer to the Lord Jesus Christ.

This story is a product of my imagination and a work of fiction. Names, characters, businesses, places, events, locales, and incidents are either the products of my imagination or in the case of actual towns, historical persons, and companies mentioned, they have been used in a fictitious manner. Any resemblance to actual persons, living or dead, or actual events is purely coincidental.

Any errors or deficiencies are my own.

Personal Testimony

I first came to know Jesus as a young teen, but before long I strayed from God and allowed my selfish desires to rule me. I sought after acceptance and love from my peers, not knowing that only God could fill my emptiness. My teen years were full of angst and misery, for me and my family. People I loved were hurt by my selfishness. My heartache was at times overwhelming, but I couldn't find the healing I desperately desired. After several runaway attempts my family was left with little choice, and they put me in a group home/residential facility where I would get the constant supervision I needed.

At that home I met a godly man called 'Big John' who tried once again to draw me back to Jesus. He would point out Matthew 11:28-30 and remind me that all I had to do to find peace was give my cares to Christ. I wanted to live a Christian life, but something kept pulling me away. The cycle continued well into adulthood. I would call out to God, but then I would turn away from Him. (If you read the Old Testament, you'll see that the nation of Israel had a similar pattern, they would call out to God and He would heal them and bring them back into their land. Then they would stray, and He would chastise them. It was a cycle that went on and on).

When I came to realize that God's love was still available to me despite all my failings, I found peace and joy that have remained with me to do this day. It wasn't God who kept walking away. He'd placed his seal on me in childhood and no matter how far I ran from Him, **He remained faithful.** When I finally recognized His unfailing love, I was made free.

2 Timothy 2:13

"If we believe not, yet he abideth faithful: he cannot deny himself."

Ephesians 4:30

"And grieve not the holy Spirit of God, whereby ye are sealed unto the day of redemption."

I let myself be drawn into His loving arms and led by His precious nail-scarred hands. He has kept me securely at His side and taught me important life lessons. Jesus has given me back the freedom I had in Christ on that day when I accepted the precious gift He'd offered. My life in Him is so much fuller than it ever was when I tried to live by the world's standards.

I implore you, if you've known Jesus and strayed, call out to Him.

If you've never known Jesus Christ as your personal Lord and Saviour. Find out what it means to have a relationship with Christ. Not religion, but a personal relationship with a loving God.

God makes it clear in His word that there isn't a person righteous enough to get to heaven on their own.

Romans 3:10

"As it is written, There is none righteous, no, not one:"

We are all sinners.

Romans 3:23

For all have sinned, and come short of the glory of God;

Death is the penalty for sin.

Romans 6:23

"For the wages of sin is death; but the gift of God is eternal life through Jesus Christ our Lord."

Christ died on the cross for our sins.

Romans 5:8

"But God commendeth his love toward us, in that, while we were yet sinners, Christ died for us."

If we confess and believe we will be saved.

Romans 10:9

"That if thou shalt confess with thy mouth the Lord Jesus, and shalt believe in thine heart that God hath raised him from the dead, thou shalt be saved."

Once we believe he sets us free.

Romans 8:1

"There is therefore now no condemnation to them which are in Christ Jesus, who walk not after the flesh, but after the Spirit."

I hope you'll take hold of that freedom and start a personal relationship with Christ Jesus.

Made in the USA
Middletown, DE
12 February 2022